A HAPPENING IN
HAWTHORNE

A HAPPENING IN HAWTHORNE

TOM A. WIGGINS

TommysTales

Contents

First Printing, 2020

Inspired by REAL people, REAL places, and TRUE events.

For: Theresa Bristow
Carl Bristow
Ted Bristow
Kenneth Bristow
Philip Bristow
Ray Bristow

Thank you for teaching our generation about family, love, passion, hard work, sacrifice, and to never be afraid of anything.

As children, we imagine that the world is a scary place.
As adults, we realize that the world is far scarier than we ever could have
imagined.

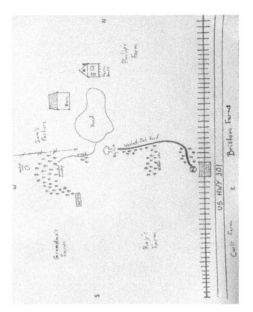

Kid Map of the part of Bristow Farms where the following events occurred.

I

You Can Always Come Home

2020

Something felt strange. I'd spent the final two years of my enlistment dreaming of returning home. I missed my family and friends. After spending most of my youth exploring the world on Uncle Sam's dime, it seemed like the logical thing to do. More importantly, it felt like the right choice. Now that I was here, I couldn't shake the feeling that something was terribly wrong.

There were no signs warning me of the fast-approaching turn, but I knew that I was getting close, so I slowed the rental car to match the speed limit. As a kid, 65 M.P.H. had always seemed too slow for this stretch of Highway 301. There was nothing here. It was just a place you had to get through to get to where you were going.

Rex Hill was nothing more than a mile or two stretch of highway. Most people think that Rex Hill is part of Hawthorne. But the old-timers would never allow that to happen. Rex Hill had always been, and will always be, its own community. No, Rex Hill was not a part of Hawthorne. Its community members identified themselves as

Hawthornians, but considered themselves something more. There were only two landmarks in Rex Hill that I could recall: Eden Baptist Church and Bristow Farms.

Some things never change, I chuckled aloud to myself considering the ridiculousness of the idea, while I sped down the southside of Rex Hill. As suddenly as expected, my turn snuck up on me. I nearly locked up the brakes on the tiny Toyota Camry, and cut the wheels hard right. As I slid off of the asphalt onto dirt and gravel, the car did not seem to want to stop. I knew the feeling. I had experienced similar turns at this exact spot a hundred times before; sometimes safely, and sometimes not.

As the Camry finally came to a halt, I was greeted by a row of rusted out mailboxes. One of them had been taped shut; excessively I thought. That mailbox would be mine. The post office had probably gotten tired cramming junk mail into an overflowing box, and had ceased service. The other boxes belonged to the remaining family who still lived on the farm. All of the mailboxes appeared to be older than me, but I could not remember them, or if that were true. On the other side of the wall of mailboxes was a ditch so deep, that I was certain the small sedan would roll several times before reaching the bottom of it.

I backed up the Camry a few feet, and corrected my trajectory on the driveway entrance. One entrance for four remaining residences. I pulled the car up the gravel, to the edge of the blacktop. The asphalt appeared to be fairly new, and signaled the beginning of the railroad crossing. There was no stop sign, crossing arms, or any other type of warning that trains regularly flew past at speeds in excess of fifty-five miles per hour. I have had enough near accidents here in my youth to know to always stop, and check both ways; multiple times.

The tracks themselves served as a warning: Do Not Enter. The tracks were steel bars on the windows to Bristow Farms. Warning those who pass by that if you get in, you may not ever get out.

I did not look both ways this time. Instead, I shifted the car into park, and cut off the engine. I sat there for a few minutes trying to recall why I left those twenty years ago. I was a young man who needed to see the world I supposed. Or was I trying to escape, but what? Why now, had I felt called to return? I exited the Camry, and walked onto the railroad tracks. I looked south down the tracks, and then I turned north. It was exactly as I recalled. The world had changed drastically in twenty years, but this, this had remained the same. Uncertain why, I began walking north up the tracks. Stepping on each railroad tie just as I had as a child. Maybe it was true, maybe nothing had changed. It felt like I was right where I belonged.

My mind was flooded with nostalgia, and suddenly, I was a boy again.

1992

Sweat fell from my brow onto the too hot to touch, cold-rolled steel. I imagined putting an ice cube into a frying pan, and looked for a sizzle. I was disappointed when there was none. I continued spacing the coins: quarter, dime, nickel, and a penny. Suddenly, I felt movement. I looked up, but didn't see anything. I didn't hear anything either. The vibrations told a different story. It was coming.

I ran through the ditch, across the dirt road, and back into the tree line. The road wasn't really a dirt road. It was more of a path for cars to follow. It consisted of two shallow ruts made from the family vehicles who used it to access the farm. To me, the ruts signified that we were all heading in the same direction; nowhere. As I crouched down, the youngest of my two sisters Tina, begged to know what I had just done, "Tommy, what is it? What did you do?"

I was just about to tell her when I heard the distant bellow. "It's a surprise, just wait," I attempted to reassure the eight-year-old girl.

From the first blast, I figured that it was about a mile away. I checked my cheap Timex watch, it was 1:15 p.m. That means it was running two minutes late. Which meant it would be coming fast. At least sixty miles per hour I guessed. If my assumptions were accurate, it should arrive in less than one minute. I started the stopwatch on my Timex.

Exactly fifty-seven seconds later the first engine tore through Bristow Farms like a tornado. Fortunately, it was a freight train. When the engine passed the crossing three hundred meters south from us, my sisters jumped up, and ran into the road. They pumped their arms begging the conductor to blast the horn. He obliged. Right in front of us, not thirty feet away, the train horn blasted, and it was enough to send the girls scurrying back into the trees. They both giggled as they rejoined me, and they tried to say something, but we were all temporarily deaf.

We loved trains. We loved the size, the power, and the purpose. Trains were always coming from, and heading somewhere exciting. Most of the trains that rumbled through Bristow Farms were freight trains, each pulling hundreds of flatbeds, boxcars, gondolas, and tank cars. My favorite were the tank cars. I always wondered what was in them. A member of our church was an ex-cartel gangster who found Jesus in prison. He said that most tank cars coming from south Florida were filled with drugs. I knew that drugs were wrong, but I also found it exciting to imagine. An occasional passenger train would zip by, but we would rarely ever see a passenger. Boxcars it seemed, carried more passengers through Florida in those days than passenger trains. Us kids would regularly wave to the freighthoppers. My Grandma fed sandwiches to these hitchhikers religiously.

The train took two minutes and nineteen seconds to pass, and I counted three hundred and sixty-seven cars. Most of the cars were empty flatbeds. I looked both ways, up and down the road. I looked back through the tree line across the fields to the house. The cars were still parked in the front yard. It seemed as safe as it was going to be. I crossed the road, climbed through the ditch, and remounted the railroad tracks. None of the coins remained on the track. I had expected them to fall. I searched through the surrounding granite rocks. Each second spent on the tracks felt like a year, and the hot rocks were blistering my skin. Misty called out from the road, "hurry up!"

I could not find a single damn coin. Where did they go? What happened to them? I searched my brain for a logical answer. Perhaps they were smashed so hard that their atoms exploded, and disappeared. Unlikely. Maybe they were welded into the rail. I inspected the rail closer, there was no indication of the coins. They must have somehow stuck to the train wheels. It was the only possible explanation.

Disappointment set in, and I rose to my feet to give up. As I turned to rejoin my sisters with nothing to show, a glimmer of light caught my eye. I looked closer, and peeking out from under a granite rock was the quarter I had placed. I snatched it up. It was bent in half, and only mildly distorted. Not exactly the outcome I was hoping for, but it was something, and something was always better than nothing.

I slid down the pile of rocks, to cut back through the ditch. When I slipped, I caught myself by leaning back into, and grabbing at the rocks for a prayer. Instead, I grabbed something unexpected. In my hand, before I saw what it was, it felt hot and heavy. It was a ten-inch railroad spike. I wondered when it had come loose, and how long it had been lying there. It made me think about how long the railroad had been there.

Bristow Farms had given the land to lay the track to the railroad company over a hundred years ago. The track ran parallel to US Highway 301, straight down the middle of Florida. Both the rail and the highway once helped Hawthorne thrive, but by the early 1990s, they had all but seemingly died.

I caught up with my sisters who were already walking the road back towards the house. "Look at what happened," I showed them the coin.

Tina took the quarter from my hand, and inspected it closely. "Why would you do that? You could have bought a coke," she cried.

"If anyone saw you, and tells Granddaddy that you were playing on the railroad tracks, he will whup you so that you can't sit for a week," Misty chimed in, "hope it was worth it."

It was.

My sisters, and I were all born in July, a year apart. I was ten, Misty was nine, and Tina was eight years old. Misty and I had dark brown hair, and tanned easily, and Tina had bright red hair, freckles, and burned easily. Most ten-year-old boys probably don't spend their days playing with their little sisters, but it was the best option out on the farm. The four cousins who also lived on Bristow Farms were all teenagers, and all Bristow's. The name difference seemed to separate us more than the age. We were outsiders. Although we were raised on Bristow Farms identically, we carried our daddy's name, we were Wiggins's. Little did I know that this would be the last summer of wonder and adventure for my sisters and I, before our personal interests or perhaps fate split us, and took us in different directions. Or, maybe it was what happened that summer that ended our daily expeditions.

For a ten-year-old boy, summer on the farm was still a lot of work, even in the 90s. I spent most of my workdays in the gardens hoeing weeds or picking vegetables. They were both the same to me. Some days were spent mowing, raking, and bailing the fields. Every evening the kids were given bushels of whatever was in season to shell, snap, pick, or shuck. The good news was that, if you could tolerate the hot box, the majority of this work could be done in front of the television. That is, until we started making a mess, or became too entranced by the picture box. Then Grandma would kick us out of the house onto the porch, or into the yard to fight yellow flies and mosquitos.

The hot box was our house. Our house was a trailer. It was a late 70s model double-wide that my uncle had given his parents, my grandparents, when he built his new house. We built a front porch onto it, that was as big as the trailer itself. The porch had a storage room that was overflowing with junk, which Grandma likened to gold. Half of the open space consisted of a large area for Grandma to do her quilting (as if she had time for a hobby), and a sitting area for folks to work, visit, or just relax and enjoy the breeze.

I once dropped a can of beans into a fire. The small tin can instantly became too hot to touch, and I was unable to retrieve it. I sat watching the can for a few moments. After the Bush's label burned off, it appeared unbothered by the heat as it nestled in the glowing embers with flames wrapping around the metal refusing to relinquish its control. Unexpectedly, the can exploded from the heat, spraying shrapnel and hot beans in every direction. The hotbox was bigger, but it was nothing more than a tin can, and the Florida heat surely was more powerful than that little fire. I knew that it was only a matter of time before the hotbox blew too.

No one in the family spent much time in the hotbox during the summer. The front porch was about as far as anyone dared to venture into the house until the sun had set. Most of the farm work occurred in the early morning, and in the late evening simply to avoid the hottest parts of the day. I preferred the early morning while the insects were still sleeping. For us kids, the midday was spent drinking from water hoses, playing in the shade, and exploring.

Spending time outdoors as a kid in the 90s was easy. We lived on a three-hundred-acre farm that may as well have been three hundred square miles to young children with unlimited imaginations. There was much to explore, and each day we expanded our boundaries a little further. Technically the only parts of the property that were off-limits was the wooded swamp and the train tracks, but when you are young, each new adventure feels like a potential trap filled with uncertainty and excitement.

That summer we had grown comfortable enough in our explorations to begin creating and began building our own little world. By June we had started construction on at least five secret forts, which were strategically placed throughout the areas of the farm which we preferred to play. Generally, these locations were just enough out of sight, to make us feel independent from any snooping adults. However, building our own independence required tools and material which we were dependent on, and also not authorized to use. Secrecy was a necessity as much as an amenity. Each fort was special in its own right, and we intentionally ensured that no two were the same.

The newest fort was also the closest to the railroad, and that is where we were headed as we veered left off of the washed-out road. All three of us were barefooted and covered in filth before noon. Our feet were toughened from days of running through the fields, jumping on bales of hay, and climbing trees. Even so, we carefully made our way into the hidden fort. Thorns, sand spurs, and stinging nettles were the only enemy we knew in those days, and we had learned to fear them.

We referred to this fort as "the hidden lair," because we believed that although it was a mere fifty yards from the road, that no one could see us in it. The fort consisted of a single, but dense strip of trees that was over a thousand feet long, but only maybe one hundred feet wide. The oak trees were enormous, and one would believe that they must be hundreds of years old. The trees towered over a flattened field as a symbol of defiance. On either side of the row of trees were planted gardens this time of year, and the rest of the year, they were simply bare fields. Just as the trees reached high into the sky, they also had enormous branches that swooped at the ground. Branches that must have gotten too heavy for the tree to bear lifting upward anymore. Branches that provided concealment, and easy access into the climbing trees for young explorers.

Although we were but small children, we found that we practically had to crawl to enter the hidden wonderland beneath. Even if the adults found the fort, they could surely never enter it, or so we believed. Immediate relief from the sun overwhelmed us as we each found a branch to relax on. I picked up a one-gallon bucket which I had filled with water from the hose at the house, and tipped it for a drink. More of the water ended up on my shirt than in my mouth, but was refreshing nonetheless.

I took a moment to admire the progress that we had made in the lair since discovering it. Several old boards had been crookedly nailed to one tree to serve as a ladder to reach a higher branch. A long-weathered rope stretched at least fifteen feet between two branches, about ten feet from the ground. Originally intended to be a tight rope bridge between the two trees, none of us had mustered the courage to attempt the crossing yet. Tina suggested that it be used as a clothesline instead. Misty, and I agreed that her idea was lame.

The most appealing feature in the fort wasn't built. Hanging from higher in the trees than we could ever hope to climb, were enormous thick vines. Vines capable of holding all three of us at the same time. When we discovered them, we imagined swinging from tree to tree like Tarzan. Although we could swing back and forth on them a little, it was nothing like the movie; however, we were determined to find a way to make the most of the vines.

Before I became too distracted by my desire to build, I announced, "oh yeah, check out what I found."

I quickly pulled the railroad spike out of my pants. It left a brown streak of rust collected in my sweaty jeans, and on my tighty-whiteys. Tina jumped down from her branch, and ran over to inspect it closer. She put her hands out asking to hold the heavy piece of metal, "what is it she asked?"

I handed her the spike, "it's a track nail," I notified the girls, maintaining my status as the big brother who knew everything.

"That nail can be used to tack anything. They use it to tack down steel rails for the trains to roll on," I enlightened them further.

By now Misty had made her way over to inspect the nail closer, although slightly less enthralled than Tina. She stated the obvious, "it doesn't look very sharp."

I snatched the nail from her hand, "this nail can go through anything," I reassured her smugly.

Tina was convinced. However, it would take proof to gain Misty's trust. "Nail it to the tree," she said, picking up the old wooden handled hammer we had been using all morning.

I took the hammer from her and replied, "ok, but only a couple of inches. We need to be able to get it out so that we can use it when we are ready."

I put the pointed end of the huge nail into the tough large bark, and instructed the girls to stand back. I swung the hammer back, then struck the nail perfectly with all of my might. The nail bounced hard off of the tree, vibrating throughout my hand, causing me to drop the hammer and the nail, and let out a yelp.

I doubled over on the ground holding my right hand tightly. Tears formed in my eyes, as my sisters dropped down beside me begging what had happened. "Did you hit your hand," Tina cried out as though I had hit hers.

I stifled the tears and stood up. I shook my right hand hard, to shake off the shock. "No, I didn't. I just wasn't expecting the recoil is all," I said, still in disbelief.

I picked up the nail and the hammer again, determined to prove the nails worth. This time I decided to tap the nail much softer to get it started. Tap tap. Tap tap. The nail did not even scratch, or begin to penetrate the bark. Frustrated, I turned to my sisters holding the nail up between us, "this nail is too big for this tree, but I have an idea, come on."

Without waiting, or looking back to see if my sisters were following me, I ran out of the lair, and onto the road, headed back toward the train tracks. Another train would be coming soon, and I wanted to make sure that it got its nail back. As I came to the crook in the road where it began to parallel the tracks, I moved into the tree line, and back into the same ditch as before. Misty and Tina caught up, and settled in behind me. Neither girl cared to ask what I was doing now; they were simply following me because that was all that they knew.

After a moment of consideration, I looked back towards the house, then up and down the road; there was no movement. I tightened my grip on the nail, and then sprinted to the track. I carefully positioned the nail directly on the track, just as I had with the coins. At first, I laid the spike across the track, finding the perfect balance so that it would not fall. Afraid of failure again, I decided to place it long ways on the track, hoping the vibrations wouldn't cause it to fall off into the rocks. Then I sprinted back to rejoin my sisters. Another train would be along shortly, and this time, I expected better results.

Misty had guessed my plan and chided me, "if you bend the nail, we won't be able to use it for anything," she had a point.

"You saw the same as I did that it's a bad nail, what could we possibly use it for?" I asked rhetorically.

Misty shrugged her shoulders, and Tina just watched the tracks. We sat there playing patiently in the ditch for fifteen minutes until I heard the first horn blast. This time the train was much closer. We all three stood up, and peeked out from behind a tree. The train rumbled past the crossing to Bristow Farms, moving just as fast as the last train. My sisters jumped out from behind the tree and begged the engineer for a blast. I stayed wrapped to the tree, my eyes fixed on the nail that waited on the tracks. I begged it with all of my being not to fall. To the girls' delight the engineer obliged their pleas with a series of short, but intense blasts of his horn.

It all happened so quickly. The train roaring by. The horn blasting its best. My sisters covering their ears, and jumping up and down in the road. And me, hiding behind my tree, searching for my nail on the tracks. Instantaneously, my sisters ran back to my position, ears covered, and giggling in glee. Until they were a few feet away from me, and their laughter turned into screams. They had realized something that I had not. Misty pointed to the tree. My eyes followed my arm to my hand which was still clinging to the tree.

There was my nail. Buried, three inches into the tree, through my hand. Blood seeped down my arm. It almost felt cool and refreshing. I looked closer and realized that although my hand was in fact nailed to the tree, it was not through the center of my hand. The nail had pierced right between my pointer finger, and my thumb. Without flinching. Without a scream. Without a tear. I pulled my hand from the tree, leaving the nail buried deep in its bark, with pieces of my flesh.

As I wrapped my shirt around my hand, it was shaking uncontrollably. The shock wore off, and I began screaming bloody murder. Of course, there was no one to hear except for my sisters. My shirt was rapidly saturating in blood. "We have to go get help," Misty stated the obvious.

Tina offered to run home, and get someone. "No, we can't. We will be in so much trouble," I rationalized aloud.

Misty pointed to my blood-soaked hand which was still shaking terribly, "Tommy, we can't hide that."

"Maybe we can say something else happened," I pleaded.

"Granddaddy had to get a shot after he stepped on that nail last winter. This nail is a lot bigger, and a lot rustier. You're gonna need a shot too," Misty made sense.

I started crying again. This time not out of pain, but out of the realization that there was no way out of this trouble which I had created. "I can't go home," I sobbed.

Tina grabbed my good hand, and with the wisdom of an eight-year-old said, "you can always go home."

2020

I climbed back into the Camry, looked both ways again, and then pulled across the railroad tracks onto Bristow Farms. Every fiber of my being screamed at once. The hair on my arm stood straight up, and I was certain that if I hadn't had product in my hair, it would too. I was home.

I turned right onto the path, parallel to the tracks, and slowly made my way down the washed-out road. As I approached the next turn, heading away from the railroad, I stopped. I looked to my left into the overgrown field of weeds, and I realized that the tree was gone. I sat for a second wondering what happened. Then I looked back toward the tracks, and realization struck. The road had been moved, maybe thirty feet. It had probably washed out, as it had a hundred times before, then the family simply started a new path. It was only fair because I had taken a new path too.

Once again, I put the car into park, and disembarked. During hurricane season this road stayed wet, and in poor condition, and that had not changed, no matter how far they moved it. I made my way to the tree line, hopping over a puddle, and trying not to get my nice slacks covered in sandspurs. I was glad to have shoes on as I recalled my days of barefooting the farm.

I searched the trees for the railroad spike, dumbfounded. Perhaps someone had come along, and taken it out. Or maybe the tree had fallen down years ago. I thought the latter unlikely, as my aging family were not very keen on heavy work. Then it occurred to me, the incident happened thirty years ago, and trees grow for far longer than boys. I began looking a little higher in the trees. Sure enough, there it was. Just like Arthur's sword, Tommy's railroad spike persevered. Almost eight feet high in the tree, and nearly completely swallowed by the bark, but it was still there. I reached up, and grabbed the spike. I'm not sure why. I certainly had not expected to be able to pull it out, but I needed to feel that it was real.

I pulled my hand down, and inspected the rusty residue which drove home the memory of my bloody hand. Then, although I had long since forgotten it, I checked out my childhood scar. It was still there too. A forgotten piece of history that was with me forever, even if I'd tried to erase it. I thought, you can always come home, but that doesn't mean that it won't be painful.

2

The Big Oak and the Bear

I continued westward on the washed-out road for a quarter of a mile until I came to the T. I stopped and peered west as far as I could recalling as many features of the landscape as possible. Even if I climbed on top of the car and squinted as hard as I could, I would not be able to see the far west-side of Bristow Farms. The road west ended here at the big oak tree.

1992

I was resigned to the yard play for two weeks following the railroad spike incident. I was just happy that I was allowed outside, and to be fair, the front yard was at least three acres of well-manicured field. Plenty of room to run around, but very little shade to escape the blistering sun or features to engage my imagination. My heart longed to explore, and play away from the house. My sisters were pretty good sports and did not wander off very far without me, opting to suffer the same punishment as their big brother.

We made up a game that we called "alligator" that we could play right in the yard, and it involved the water sprinkler. One person was the alligator, and the gator had to stay in the river where the sprinkler worked its way back and forth. The river was designated by the ruts in the ground that had become the driveway of sorts. In the river were two "fish". For the fish, we used small sticks. The other two players had to start from opposite riverbanks, retrieve the fish, and make it to the other bank without being "eaten", or tagged, by the alligator. If you were tagged, then you became the alligator. The game goes on until a gator can tag both players on the same crossing, which is the only way to win. A simple game, but it ate up hours of our days, and our energy.

We were playing alligator, Tina had been the gator for a long time, and was getting frustrated. Grandma came out and stood watching us play, which was a rare occurrence. There simply were not enough hours in the day for the woman who worked full time, ran a large household, a farm, and was raising her second set of kids. We were all trying our best to impress Grandma with our alligator skills when she finally piped up, "do any of you want to go on a walk with me?"

Grandma was not a large woman, but she had an imposing stature. By sixty-three years old her hair had turned solid white, and she had shriveled to barely eclipse five feet tall. She carried herself so that everyone knew that she meant business. Her face was kind but told the story of a woman who had endured much and could accomplish anything.

None of us had ever known Grandma to do any exercise beyond the demands of the family and the farm. I felt as though she had just offered to take me to the fair. The opportunity to escape my punishment was even greater than alligator.

First, we walked to the south end of the farm. There is nothing overly exciting this way, and it is only perhaps a quarter of a mile. Grandma had brought us each an apple to offer to the horses. The horse pasture is more than ten acres so as my grandmother walked the path, we were hugging the barbed wire fence, trying to coax the horses to come to us. They appeared content under the single pear tree in the center of the field, and Grandma gave us her daily notification that the horses were eating up all of her good pears. We ended up just tossing the fruit towards the horses as we turned around, and headed north.

It was a relief, that when we returned to the front yard, Grandma didn't turn towards the house, instead maintaining a northerly course. I didn't particularly want to play anymore alligator, and I was hoping to be able to check on the fort.

The washed-out road was a quarter of a mile north of the front yard. As we walked past gardens overflowing with work to be done, we did our best to distract Grandma, lest our adventure end up working the fields. We were all talking over one another as we approached the big oak tree at the end of the washed-out road.

Suddenly, Grandma shouted, "run home!"

Confused, I looked up to Grandma who was trying to usher us backward in a frantic. I noticed a black reflection in her glasses, and I spun around. Leaning against the big oak tree was the largest bear I could ever imagine. I joined the urgency to retreat. As I brought up the rear, I looked behind us, but nothing followed.

We made it home to tell our tale to my grandfather, and Uncle Mark. They grabbed the shotgun and headed to the big oak. I was allowed to tag along so that I could point out exactly where we saw the bear. It was apparent that neither of the men believed me, or Grandma. We left the road and walked into the garden in order to see around the big full branches of the tree. Sure enough, the bear was still sitting right where we had seen it.

Granddaddy inched toward the bear. Uncle Mark and I expected the bear to wake up angry, and charge at any second. Once he was about ten feet from the bear, Granddaddy pulled the trigger. The bear didn't move an inch. "He missed," I whispered to Uncle Mark.

"I don't think so. Even if he missed, the bear would have woken," he stated the obvious.

Granddaddy crept closer to the bear until he was less than five feet away, and then fired again. Still no movement. Granddaddy lowered his gun and turned to us, "it's dead."

I followed Mark to join his father. I had never been to a zoo and had only seen bears in books. The bear was taller than me sitting down. Just as the two men began discussing how the bear might've gotten there, my cousin John pulled up on his four-wheeler.

John was my older cousin. He must've been sixteen at least because he drove a big muddin truck that everyone called "Big Blue", and I was obsessed with its enormous tires, which were taller than me. John told us the story of his bear. He was hauling it home on the four-wheeler, but it kept falling off. So, he leaned it against the tree and ran home to get some rope. I shared my story about Grandma's walk, and Mark shared the story of shooting a dead bear; twice.

3

The Pond

Just west of the big oak tree was one of a million barbed wire fences that were stretched throughout Bristow Farms. We pretended that it held the cattle, but all it really did was discourage them from going wherever they wanted all of the time. I looked over the barbed wire to see that the pond was currently full; an indicator of a wet Spring.

The pond looked better than I remembered it. The only thing that the pond was good for was cooling the cattle on one hundred-degree days. The cows would pile into the small pond, and just stand there in reprieve from the blistering heat. I tried to imagine how much cooler our summers might have been if the pond were swimmable. The water was too dirty and too dangerous. The only thing I ever saw, bigger than a tadpole, move in the water, were moccasins.

We tried to stock the pond with fish once. I don't think that any survived. At least I never caught one. For some reason that I never understood, the pond was brimming with tadpoles. My sisters and I would catch them by the thousands, and keep them in five-gallon buckets. We imagined all of the fun that we could have with a thousand frogs. We never produced even one.

1992

My punishment was lifted after the bear scare. The new rule was that we had to check-in at the hotbox every hour or so. Unfair we thought, but tolerable.

Weeks of restriction to the yard provided ample opportunity to dream up new ideas. Those who cannot do; daydream. We also found ourselves wandering into the house more for drinks, and snacks. Normally we would be so busy, and far from home, that we made do with whatever was closest. Usually, the water hose.

My grandparents didn't buy soda or juice. I never saw my Grandma drink anything other than water. Granddaddy drank an occasional glass of sweet tea made with fake sugar. The one drink that we always had plenty of on hand was milk.

You might think that living on a farm, and cattle ranch, that having an abundance of milk seems logical. However, none of the Bristow Farms had a dairy farm. Never-the-less, we always had at least two gallons of milk in the refrigerators. I think that the main reason for my punishment being lifted, was to get us out of, and away from the house before we drank, and ate everything in the kitchen.

We drank so much milk during those two weeks that there was a pile of empty milk jugs on the front porch, waiting to be hauled off. My sisters and I scooped up the thirteen jugs and hid them in the old shed near the creek. Initially, we didn't know what we would use them for, but we knew that anything in abundance was useful.

The old shed appeared to be piecemealed together. In the center, there was poured concrete that had been poorly finished and was stained with oil splotches. Several rusty chains hung from a large beam that ran the width of the concrete, ten feet high. We called this part of the shed, the carport. It was where Granddaddy worked on engines from the cars, tractors, and lawnmowers. Left of the carport was another section of the shed which stored all manner of farm tools, and the small red International tractor. Right of the carport were stacks of lumber and cinder blocks. Behind the carport, in equivalent size to the three front sections, was storage. The storage section was filled with junk and a few hidden treasures. The entire shed had a tin roof which we would often find ourselves standing under during afternoon thunderstorms. The shed stood between Uncle Mark's trailer and the creek.

Misty and I were sitting in the creek trying to keep cool on the hot July day when Tina came skipping across the field with two more jugs in her hands. The creek was no more than a foot deep and was blood red. Grandma once told us the red came from the tannic acid in the leaves. Water flowed from the swamp to the pond from this creek, and was very low flow, except for when it rained. We had built a dam to slow the flow even more in this section and create a small pool that was just big enough for the three of us to sit in and splash a bit.

"I have an idea," Tina said louder than she needed to as she approached, holding up the jugs.

Misty and I looked at Tina waiting for her idea, and Tina looked at us waiting for us to ask. I took the bait, "ok, what do ya got?" I asked.

"We can use the jugs to float on the water," Tina said as she dropped one jug into the creek.

Not amused, I pushed the jug under the water, "good idea," I responded sarcastically.

She dropped the other jug into the creek too, "but can you sink both?" she asked.

I was still sitting in the water, and try as I may, I could not push the two jugs under at the same time. I stood up and used all of my weight to make the plastic touch the creek bed. I stood upright and smiled at Tina. I got the point. If we put all of the jugs together, they would be able to float us. Not in the creek obviously, but across the one farm feature which had eluded us; the pond.

The pond had taunted us for years. A big body of water that could not be swam in, could not be fished in, and yet beckoned us to play. Now we had an idea. A way to enjoy the water, without the dangers of actually being in the mud and muck. No ear infections, and no water moccasin bite. A failproof plan.

We made our plans and collected supplies. First, we needed a floor. We found an old half-rotten piece of plywood that was six feet long, and four feet wide in the shed. We were certain that it would not be missed. Although it was thin, it was still fairly difficult for three children to handle. We figured that there would be no way to move it once it was fully constructed, so we would have to put it all together at the pond.

We slid the piece of plywood along the ground. We took the best route we could think of to avoid being seen. We snuck between the wood-line and the garden. When we made it to the barbed wire fence, we didn't cross it. We moved the plywood into the woods, near the creek at the mouth of the pond. We hoped that my Uncle Philip wouldn't spot the plywood hidden here when he checked on the cows.

Then we gathered all of the milk jugs and brought them to the pond as well. We laid out the jugs on the plywood. Misty was the first to notice, "we don't have enough."

"We could space them out," I suggested.

It wasn't a risk that we were willing to take. We decided to wait. We only needed a few more jugs to cover the entire plank of wood. A few more days at the most, and we would have all the jugs we needed. We used this time to find a glue gun in the shed, and start gluing the jugs to the wood. I had no idea if this would work. Would the glue bond the plastic to the wood?

As we glued each jug to the wood, it certainly seemed to be sticking. The question remained; would it hold. Minutes after we finished gluing the last jug that we had to the board, the sky opened up, and the flood gates opened. Frantically, we pulled the wood up away from the creek in hopes that it would not be prematurely swept into the pond.

We ran under the tin covered shed, soaked from the downpour. "Well, that was a waste of time," I grumbled as I rung out my shirt.

"What do you mean?" Tina asked naively.

"The glue isn't gonna be able to set in this weather. We will be lucky if we can save any of the materials," I cried out.

It was one of those afternoon Florida rainstorms that could drown a bullfrog. It came fast and hard and did not seem to want to let up.

Within minutes the front yard had absorbed as much moisture as it possibly could, and the entire field turned into a shallow waterhole.

When the lightning stopped, we played in the front yard using the grass as a slip and slide. There would be no returning to the pond today, it was too wet and too late. It was the perfect ending to a hot day, and soon we had forgotten all about our lost raft.

A few days later I saw Tina leaving the house with two milk jugs. I had forgotten all about our raft, but Tina was still building. I joined her on the walk to the pond, but I told her to expect the worst. If the raft were still there at all, it would be in pieces.

When we arrived, Misty was already there. She was dragging the raft back down to the creek. To my surprise, it seemed to be fully intact. "How did you fix it? my question was aimed at Misty.

"I didn't. This is how I found it," she responded pointing to the raft.

It looked unaffected by the storm. I crouched down and tried to move the jugs that we had glued. They did not move. I could not believe it. The dream was alive. We just had to finish attaching a few more jugs, and we would be floating on the pond. By the end of the week, I would be a sea captain.

In three short days, we were ready to sail. The raft was in the water and floating. My first thought was, *I am a genius.* Then I recalled, no, *my sister is a genius.* As if on cue, "how are we going to get it to move?" Tina asked.

She was right. It would be difficult to set sail without a sail. "I know, we need a paddle," I exclaimed as I took off running toward the shed.

I returned moments later with a short one by four. My sisters checked it out and pushed around the water with it. "Ok, you guys ready?" I stated more than asked as I boarded the raft.

The raft immediately bobbed beneath the water but raised back up. I jumped off of the raft back onto the shore. "I don't think it is going to hold all three of us," I cautioned.

"We should test it. Tina, you weigh the least amount, so you should go first," I encouraged her.

After all, it was her idea.

Tina took the paddle from me and looked at Misty nervously. We each took one of her hands and helped her onto the platform. It bobbed a little but did not submerge the way it had when I jumped onto it. It was floating! Tina's nerves were overcome with excitement. She began paddling. The raft was working as she moved away from the shore toward the middle of the pond.

Every foot further she paddled the more jealous I became. Misty and I started calling Tina back so that we could take a turn. She kept paddling in the same direction, not knowing how to turn the raft. "Paddle to the other side, we will meet you over there," I hollered as Misty, and I ran around the pond.

She had reached the middle of the pond, and Misty and I were still cheering at the enormous success of our creation. Suddenly, Tina stopped paddling and stood up straight. She looked directly at us, but with a graveness that I will never forget. All of the excitement and happiness were drained from her face, and replaced with sheer fear. Then she looked back towards the house for a second. Then back in our direction.

"What's wrong?!" I hollered, "keep paddling."

She looked visibly confused standing on the raft, holding the paddle in both of her hands. She began shaking, and the raft responded to her movement. Suddenly, she fell into the water. As she re-emerged, I realized that I could not see the raft anymore. It had sunk. "Tina, swim to us!" we begged her.

You don't drown by falling in the water, you drown by staying there. I was forced to recall the line from a book Grandma had recently read to me. I thought, as long as she keeps moving, she would be fine.

As she swam to us, I had the epiphany. Although we had glued the jugs to the wood, and they had bonded well, we had not glued the caps to the jugs. My guess was that the caps popped off under the pressure, and caused the jugs to fill up, sinking the raft. Stupid mistake, I thought, but an easy fix.

Luckily Tina was probably a better swimmer than I was. The water was thick, and difficult to push through. As she exited the pond, Misty and I helped pull her out, as her feet sank with each step getting stuck in the mud every time. Tina's bright red hair looked impossibly filthy and matted from the short swim in the pond. Then I noticed that under the muddy water and tears streaking down her face, she was as white as a ghost, and she was shivering violently.

How in the world could she be shivering, I thought? It's ninety-eight degrees in the shade, and the water is uncomfortably warm. As quickly as I dismissed the possibility that she was cold a new horror set in. She'd been bit. It all added up. Her actions on the raft, jumping off and swimming to us, her current state. I knew my sister had been bitten by a water moccasin.

Tina had been out of the water for fifteen seconds, and still not said a word. I grabbed her by her shoulders, and for the first time, she looked directly at me. "Are you bit?" I cried.

She only looked at me long enough to hear my words, and then she turned her head, again staring off in the distance to the north. She did not answer with words, but merely shook her head "no."

I was not convinced. This was a serious thing, even a child understood the severity of a poisonous snake bite. Just last fall a neighbor from the next farm up had been bitten by a snake. He was wearing boots and killed the snake not realizing it had bitten him. When he got home, he sat down in his recliner to watch the news, never taking his boots off. He fell asleep. He never woke up again.

By now Misty had joined in my hysteria, but Tina was still unresponsive. Misty and I were checking Tina for bite marks. I started by searching high, and Misty searched low. Then we switched. We could not find any bite marks or indications of injury. We were forced, at least momentarily, to believe that our sister was not injured.

Misty and I both stood facing our youngest sister. She still seemed to be in a state of shock. Neither of us could understand why. Yes, the raft was gone, but she could swim, and now she was safe. Finally, Misty had enough. She put a hand on each of Tina's shoulders and shook her, "what's wrong!" she demanded.

Tina then calmly, and slowly turned her head slightly to the right looking directly at Misty. It almost seemed as though she were looking through her. "She is calling me to come home," Tina told Misty softly.

That's why she stood up and looked back toward the house, I thought. "Crap, I didn't hear them. We better run," I pulled Tina's hand to go.

She yanked her hand from mine. "Not our home," there was a slight pause, "that one," she said as she pointed north to the old abandoned house."

4

The Place Where It All Began

2020

I needed to turn south, towards the old run-down trailer. I had made this trip to conduct an assessment of what needed to be done to clean up my portion of the farm that had been left to me by my grandmother who had passed away in 2014. I knew that there was a lot of work to be done, and intended to at least get started. To build for the future, I would first have to get rid of most of the past, and I imagined that would not be easy.

Something beckoned me to turn north instead. It would only take a moment to have a look around I thought, as I shifted the car back into drive, and made the right turn. I crept along slowly, inspecting the scenery for change. The pond was to my left, to the west, and glistened in the sunlight. I crossed the drainage ditch which relieved the pond and kept it from overflowing. There were cows on my right enjoying the shade trees. Most of the herd were in the meadows doing what they do best; grazing.

Straight ahead I spotted the Green House. The only difference was that the house was no longer green. My entire life had been spent think-ing that it was impossible to find an uglier color to paint that small cin-der block house, but now I saw that I was wrong. It had been painted, for lack of a better description, poop brown. I imagined an uncle paint-ing the walls with buckets of cow manure, and laughed to myself.

I turned west in the yard and parked the car. The cattle gate was closed, and I rested a foot on the bottom bar, and leaned over the top rail as if I were a rancher or a cowboy in a Hollywood film. I looked west over another cattle field, and spotted a dozen cows way off in the distance. There once stood an enormous multi-level barn in this gated area, but there was no sign of it now, as if it had never existed. To the left, the steel cattle chutes still sat where they had been installed decades before I was born. I knew that if there were still cattle on the farm, that the chutes were still being used to tag and treat the cows. Between the chutes and the pond, a large grain bin sat, but it looked empty. There was a time that it was covered and sat next to a smaller storage area, that was typically overflowing with cattle feed.

I looked south and realized that I could see my childhood home in the distance. Thirty years ago, it would not have been possible to see around the original Bristow homestead.

The first house built on Bristow Farms was framed in 1880. Its foun-dation consisted of a couple of dozen concrete blocks, and the rest of the house was milled timber from the property. Although it absolutely would not meet modern-day building codes, the house stood for over one hundred years until 2003 when a strong storm finally blew the house over.

This was the house my grandmother, and all of her siblings were born in. The house had a small back porch and a slightly larger front porch. If you tried, you could see the pond from either porch. The small house was two stories tall and had a brick chimney that reached up the north wall. I doubt that the house had ever been painted. The down-stairs consisted of a kitchen that also served as a dining room, and a wooden wall separated it from the living room. Upstairs were two small bedrooms that the family of eight slept in. By today's standards of living, the house doesn't seem like much, but it served its purpose as a safe place to lie your head following the civil war (the shooting may have stopped in 1865, but the war didn't end in Hawthorne until well into the 1880s) until I left for Afghanistan in 2001. The original Bristow homestead was built before the town of Hawthorne was founded in 1881.

1992

It took a couple of days for Tina to shake what she referred to as *the calling*. During this time, she remained distant, no matter where we were or what we were playing. I would constantly notice her looking in the direction of the old tired farmhouse. Misty and I still could not understand exactly what had happened. Tina had heard someone calling her, but neither of us had heard it on the shore. We didn't understand how it could be possible. Tina described the calling as low and soft. As though whoever was calling her, were standing right in front of her.

Misty and I had both asked her a hundred times what the call was. Tina replied the same every time, *come home*. Here is where she lost us. If the calling was to come home, and it wasn't coming from the hot box, and she believed it was coming from the farmhouse then: 1. How come we couldn't hear it, since Misty and I were closer? 2. How could the calling be soft because the house was more than a football field away from the center of the pond?

Tina could not rationalize the calling any further. She wasn't lying. It was apparent that she believed that she heard something. Misty and I however could not be certain what she heard, or why she heard it, and we had not.

Three days after the calling, Tina seemed pretty much back to normal. Grandma gave us a tasking to go pick blackberries. Blackberries were our favorite thing to pick. Blackberries did not grow in planted rows in a garden. We had to hunt for them because they grow wild. Blackberries can be found all over Bristow Farms, along the fence lines, and in the woods. We were each given a one-gallon bucket, and the expectation was to return with the bucket filled. Returning a full bucket was always difficult because we all loved eating the sweet berries right off of the thicket.

The only two downsides to picking blackberries were thorns and snakes. No matter how carefully we tried to pick the berries, all of our fingers and clothes would be shredded by the thickets. Blackberry picking usually ended when we spotted the snake. It was as inevitable as the afternoon rainstorm, every time we ever picked blackberries, a snake would find us. Luckily, we were always careful enough that no one ever got bitten while picking berries. It would have ruined the fun of berry picking forever.

We had worked our way from the western wood line, across the creek, and all the way back around the barn, and heading to the fence line on the eastern side of the pond; near the old farmhouse. I couldn't see my own face, but both of my sisters had blackberry juice smeared from their mouths to their ears. We were all likely fueled up on a sugar high from eating too many berries. Too high to even realize that we were walking right past the old farmhouse.

Tina and Misty moved on to the fence line picking the next batch of berries. I lingered behind. In the front yard of the farmhouse was a large pecan tree, which was already dropping thousands of nuts on the ground. I picked up a handful of pecans and joined my sisters at the fence. While they continued picking, I began throwing pecans at the pond, trying to make them skip. Almost as though it were an instant reminder of the incident earlier in the week, Tina's head shot up. She looked to the pond, and then focused all of her attention on the farmhouse. "It's calling," she told us quietly.

Misty and I both looked to the farmhouse. We were as quiet as we could possibly be. It sounded as though I could hear every movement happening on the farm in that instant, but I couldn't hear the calling. Tina looked scared stiff and said, "there it is again, can you hear it?"

I looked at Misty, and she looked at me. We could not hear any calling. Tina was near tears again, and I put my arm around her to assure her that there was no calling. As though something had read my mind, there was a movement in the window followed by a horrific screech.

All three of us were already moving. Running full speed south towards the hot box. We had all left our buckets behind. When I reached the big oak at the end of washed-out road, I stopped. My sisters caught up with me quickly. "What was that?" Misty asked desperately.

I was young, and in incredible shape, but the air was thicker than Grandma's tomato soup. I struggled to catch my breath. "Ok, I definitely heard that," I conceded while huffing.

"Did you hear it?" Tina was alert, which occurred to me as a good thing.

Misty answered first, "it sounded like a big cat."

I tried to rationalize, "a bobcat maybe," I suggested.

Tina reacted calmly, "it wasn't a cat, I saw a person."

"Wait, what?! How could you tell it was a person? It moved across the window so fast," I tried to correct Tina.

"I saw her that day," she looked me in the eyes, "from the pond."

"You saw someone in the house the other day?" I was confused.

"Yes. She was calling me to come home," Tina acted as though this were old information.

"You didn't say anything about seeing anyone before," scoffed Misty, "you're lying!"

Once again, Tina calmly and logically replied, "I was afraid that you would want to look in the house."

"Maybe we should take a look. I am sure there is an explanation," I offered.

"She scares me," is all Tina responded with.

"Who scares you?" I wondered aloud.

"The lady in the window who calls," Tina said as though it should have been obvious.

Misty and I knew better. It wasn't that we didn't trust that our baby sister believed that she saw a lady in the house, but it just wasn't possible. There were only three women on the farm, and we knew for certain Aunt Sarah and Grandma were at work. I wasn't sure where my Aunt Tojuanna (Toe-wanna) was, but I highly doubted that she would ever step foot in that rickety run-down house.

"You say *the lady* as though you don't recognize her," I deduced to Tina.

Tina shook her head, "I don't."

"So, you are saying that there is a stranger living in that old house?" Misty asked incredulously.

Again, Tina slowly nodded her head, and tears began to swell in her eyes again, "no."

Frustration began to overcome me, "Tina, you are not making any sense."

She began to sob, "I don't think that she is alive."

2020

Even as a young boy I was never one to believe in ghosts and spirits. I enjoyed any scary movies that I could sneak in on my uncle's satellite when he was at work. Monsters, spirits, and ghosts were all pretend. Made up to entertain and delight those who could stomach a story. I looked back over the sun-drenched fields and thought if the cows aren't spooked, then why should I be.

5

Wel-Come Home

Unexpectedly, a heavy hand landed on my shoulder. I was shaken so that I nearly fell off of the gate. Before I could turn around a familiar voice filled the air, "Tommy? I thought that was you!"

"Sorry to sneak up on ya. I saw a strange car turn up this way, and figured I had better come check it out," Uncle Ray explained.

Uncle Ray lived on the south-east corner of Bristow Farms, as he had his entire life. If I had taken an immediate left after crossing the rail-road tracks, I would have entered his front yard. Uncle Ray is really my great uncle. He is my grandmother's youngest brother. To give you an idea of their age difference, Ray was born the same year as my grand-mother's oldest son.

Ray was now pushing seventy years old, but he had the energy of a seventeen-year-old. He was one of those old men who could not sit still. He seemed to speed up with age. It was as though the less time he had remaining in the world, the more he wanted to get done. I admired his spirit, and willingness to help anyone with any job. He was average in stature, and his hair had long since completely whitened. His most dis-tinguishing feature was his quick twangy speech, which was far more pronounced than all of his brothers' slow southern drawl.

"I saw ya stop at the big oak, and then finally turn up this way. You looked lost. You haven't been gone for that long have ya?" Uncle Ray joshed.

Uncle Ray was known for having the best sense of humor in the family. His demeanor was annoying for some folks, but I always enjoyed his wit and laughter. I embraced the aging man, "how have you gotten thinner since retirement?" I poked back.

"Less sweet tea and fried chicken," he said with a rare seriousness.

"Oh, sweet tea and fried chicken, that sounds amazing right now," I let him know that I was serious as well with my expression.

"Well, it's a little early in the evenin for chicken, but I bet we can rassle you up some tea at the house, come on up and say hi to Tojuanna," Ray commanded.

I hated to cut my tour of the farm short, but I couldn't turn down a glass of ice-cold sweet tea as hot as it was. As we pulled into his yard, Ray's wife, my Aunt Tojuanna came out onto the porch to greet me. Armed with a sweet hello, and lingering hug she welcomed me home and invited me inside for refreshments.

All three of us were trying to talk over one another engaged in small talk as Tojuanna disappeared into the kitchen. Excited for the glass of tea, I was eager with anticipation. She returned a moment later with a big bowl. "Dang, have I been up north so long that I've forgotten how we drink sweet tea down here?" I asked, inciting raucous laughter.

"I hope not, but I just want to make sure you're real thirsty for that sweet tea," she said as she handed me the bowl with a knowing smile.

Excitement overwhelmed me as I spied the inside of the bowl. "Boiled peanuts?!" I nearly shouted in glee.

We sat and talked for a long time as the couple caught me up on the local family news and other happenings in Hawthorne. I shared what I had been up to playing Army all these years. Lastly, I told them my plans for my part of the farm; to clear, and rebuild something that we could be proud of and use.

After an hour or more of shooting the breeze, I reminded them that I wanted to recon and assess the property before it got too late. We all stood up, and I headed toward the door. "Oh, we almost forgot, we have something for you," Tojuanna said as she wandered into a back room.

Ray and I worked our way onto the porch as he pointed out some ongoing projects he was working on in the yard. We walked to the side yard, and I spotted something else I had forgotten about; another old farmhouse.

I had never spent much time poking around on Ray's property, but I recalled the old pump well. I couldn't believe it was not only still there, but working. Fifty feet beyond the well was the house that it was originally meant for. It was still standing straight and looked in relatively good condition. "Uncle Ray, how old is that house?" I asked.

"Oh, I don't remember. Sometime around the turn of the century, I reckon," he said.

"Wow, have you been inside recently?" my interest was peaking.

"Oh yeah, that house is in good shape boy. I was just in there this morning getting some things out. We mostly use it for storage now," he informed me.

I was amazed, but also curious. "Has anything strange ever happened in that house," I asked, trying not to offend, or sound too suspicious.

Before he could answer, Aunt Tojuanna returned with the gift she had been searching for. Before she could even hand it to me, uncle Ray began explaining its specialness, "that's a picture of your mama when she was a little girl, and that's her mama and her daddy, and our brother Carl there," he pointed them out one by one.

Uncle Ray referred to my Grandma as my mama since she had raised me. The lines in our family were very blurred. It didn't bother me at all. In fact, it made me feel closer to everyone than I might have been otherwise. I'm not sure how many other people refer to their great uncles as Uncle, but my actual uncles were more like older brothers.

It was an incredible picture, and I could not remember ever having seen it before. It was taken in black and white, and it must have been shot during the great recession, sometime in the mid-1930s. As I was admiring the great piece of history I had been given, Uncle Ray continued.

"Now you might not remember it, but there used to be an old farm-house up there by the pond. It blew down, oh I dunno, has to be at least ten years ago now. That was the house your mama grew up in. I made the frame here, out of wood from that house. I used a router to make this edge here," Ray continued but my thoughts drowned out his voice.

I felt overwhelmed with emotions. To be holding such a sentimental piece of my family's history was almost more than I could bear. But there was more history here than even Uncle Ray knew. More moving than the frame was the picture. The youngest picture of Old Grandma that I had ever seen. Old Grandma was the name that we called my Grandmas' mother when we were young. She died when I was five or six years old. The young woman in the picture looked very familiar; I had seen her before.

My thoughts were interrupted by Aunt Tojuanna's hand as she took the frame from me. "Your Uncle Ray tried to engrave the back of the frame for you," she made a silly face that I had seen her make a million times before.

As I flipped the frame over to read the inscription, Uncle Ray explained, "it was supposed to read *welcome home*, but I messed up and had to cut it short..."

When I saw the inscription, I nearly dropped the frame. The top of the frame read *Come*, and the bottom of the frame read *Home*.

1992

After thirty minutes of back and forth, we decided not to go back to the farmhouse. All of us were a little too freaked out by what had just happened. I was convinced it was a bobcat we heard and saw, but my sisters were not as sure as I was. I was thirsty anyway, so we went home and got a drink from the water hose, then played alligator for the rest of the afternoon.

Bobcats were familiar on Bristow Farms. Besides deer and maybe turkeys, bobcats were the most commonly seen creatures lurking the wood line. It seemed like every season we would end up with a bobcat or two in the 'coon traps we set. Although bobcats are roughly the same size as raccoons, and twice the size of a house cat, they are built for agility and speed. Bobcats were considered an endangered species in Florida in the early 90s, and as such, were not to be harmed. We learned the hard way that you can't just release a bobcat from a 'coon trap. Bobcats are scrappy creatures, and will not hesitate to attack if they feel threatened. We learned to leave the bobcat in the trap for several days, until it was dehydrated and starving, and then release it. That way, when the trap is open, they are too weak and thirsty to attack. The bobcats always ran for water and safety. If a bobcat were trapped or living in the farmhouse, I was unsure how we could get it out.

When Grandma got home, she did what she always does. Changed out of her good work clothes into her farm work clothes, and set to pulling peanuts. My sisters sat off to the side picking the peanuts off of the bushels and throwing them into the buckets. I was barely strong enough to pull most of the bushes from the ground myself, and so Grandma, and I worked together pulling peanuts from the garden. The girls were giggling about something to themselves at the end of the row, and Grandma was loading bushels into my arms to take to them. "Are the blackberries good?" Grandma seemed to ask out of nowhere.

She read the look on my face as I realized that we had left our buckets up by the farmhouse. "Tommy, don't tell me that ya'll ate all of the berries?" she scolded more than asked.

"No ma'am," I was glad to report that we hadn't.

"We just left the buckets up near the pond," I shrunk down a little at her scowl.

"How many times do I have to tell you children, to take care of my stuff," she reprimanded me as she rapped me on the bare legs with a bushel.

Nothing in this world hurts worse than being spanked with a bushel of peanuts.

"Ya'll go get em," she commanded, but we were already moving, "you better hope they are still there," she shouted after us as if they might have walked off.

We ran nearly half a mile, back to where we had left the berries. As we approached the buckets, none of us were looking at them. The house had our full attention. The sun was getting low, and it somehow made the creepy farmhouse look spookier than it had ever looked before. "Are you thinking what I'm thinking?" I asked the girls.

It did not appear that they were. I was determined to look in the house, even if it were dangerous. I had to know if someone was squatting, or something was living in there, which seemed to be the most rational explanation. I began walking closer to the house and turned to make sure that the girls were with me. They weren't. "Come-on stop being scaredy pants," I tried to entice them.

Misty budged, but Tina did not. One was enough I thought. I didn't want to be alone if I were attacked by an adult or a bobcat. "Tina, you stand guard out here. If something happens, you run get Grandma, ok?" I instructed.

Tina nodded her head in agreement, and it was apparent that Misty understood why I let Tina off of the hook. We jumped up on the porch. The entire house was littered with junk, and filled with trash. There were books older than my Grandma, and coke bottles from the forties. It occurred to me for the first time, that if this old house weren't haunted, it would make a pretty cool clubhouse. We had not considered it before because Uncle Philip spent a lot of time in the barn, and as a younger man, he liked to yell. To be fair he mainly yelled at us for playing on his equipment, and in his freshly baled hay.

The stairs inside of the house were collapsed. We were certain that there was no one upstairs. "There ain't no way that anyone is living in this pile of trash," Misty observed aloud.

Her observation was as honest as any that I could derive myself. It cemented my belief that there was a wild cat in the house. It was just a coincidence that we saw something in the house at the same time that Tina heard the calling. However, that still did not explain the calling itself. We rummaged through the old belongings for a few minutes, until I realized that Grandma would whup me if we took any longer. It was obvious that there was no one in the house.

I was about to call Misty to leave when she poked me, and quietly said, "Tommy, look," she was pointing upward.

I looked up to the kitchen ceiling. Carved in the old wooden beam read the words *Come Home.*

6

If Ghosts are Real, then
Monsters are Too

2020

This time when I reached the big oak tree, I made the turn south to-wards my house. This part of the property was primarily empty acreage now. There were no endless rows of garden or pretty horses to admire. Everything was overgrown, and it was apparent that the grass had not been mowed in quite a long time. Other than a few fallen trees, nearly everything else appeared the same.

On my property remained three rundown double-wide trailers. The homes were literally imploding. I imagined that none of the houses had incurred any type of maintenance since my Granddaddy came down with the sickness in 1998. He passed away in 2001, leaving my ailing grandmother to run the farm alone. By 2001 there hadn't been anything more than a small garden in years.

Grandma was the gardener, and Granddaddy was the repairman. He could fix just about anything that you could break. He knew a lot about engines, but not much about farming. He was handy enough that he could accomplish the tasks as Grandma directed. However, it was always Grandma leading any farming initiative.

Grandma was the Bristow. She was the oldest of the remaining Bristow generation. Her side of the family had been working this land longer than anyone could remember. Every time the town would talk about extending city limits to include Bristow Farms, she would remind folks *the Bristows were here before Hawthorne, and we will still be here after Hawthorne too.*

Granddaddy was a Brady. The Bradys weren't from around these parts. The Bradys hailed from southern Georgia. As a young man, Granddaddy was a sapper. He would walk in the woods, and drain sap from the trees. Some sap was used to make syrup, and others were used to make adhesives. Granddaddy was never a hunter, but he liked living on the farm for the privacy and the woods that reminded him of his youth.

There always seemed to be an unspoken tension between the Bradys and the Bristows. I joked on several occasions that we were trying to mimic the Hatfields and McCoys. I often wondered if the Bristow side was worried that the Brady side was trying to steal their legacy; the farm. Grandma and Granddaddy had six children, five boys, and one girl. The lone girl was my mother. One of the Brady boys died as a teenager in an automobile accident. Two of the Brady boys lived on the farm most of their lives.

After I left for the Army in 2001, my Uncle Mark moved from the next-door trailer, in with his mother. He was able to help her get around the house, with her medicine, and take her to her doctor's appointments. Never being treated himself for his diabetes, Mark had his own ailments which slowed him down more than the average fifty-year-old man.

Uncle Mark was an untrained academic and could discuss just about any subject you might desire for hours. He read the encyclopedia every day and stayed on top of current events. However, Mark was not much of a handyman and did not make a lot of money in his business mowing lawns. As such, the property slipped into despair from 2001 to his death in 2018. Presently, there was a lot to do to make the property livable, and usable again.

Against my better judgement I entered the trailer I was raised in; the hot box. The last time I had set foot in the hotbox, it was unbearable. Filth and clutter are the nicest ways to put the state the house was in. Now, the trailer had been sitting empty for two years. The family had picked over the belongings for anything that they believed was valuable. All that remained was junk, trash, and some pictures hanging on the walls.

The trailer had a dank smell, but for the most part, looked the same as I remembered it. The wood panel walls still hugged the studs tightly, but in several places, I spotted mold infestations in the ceiling. It seemed that every room in the house had at least one hole in the floor, where the particle board had given way to something sturdier. I stepped carefully in an effort to avoid falling through unexpectedly.

I began taking the pictures off of the wall one by one, trying to remember when they were taken, and relive a simpler time. I reached for the next frame, when I realized, it was the same picture that Uncle Ray had just given me. A picture I had never seen before today, I had now seen in two different locations.

The frame looked the same too. It was crafted from aged wood with large lifelines that you could not find in lumber stores these days. The wood was aged gray, and unpainted, except for a single splotch of green substance that I couldn't make out. I examined the picture on the wall for a long time. I tried to focus on my grandmother as a young child, and appreciate the significance of the photo. No matter how hard I tried, my attention kept reverting to the beautiful young lady holding the little girl.

Old Grandma was not old at all in this picture, but there was already a story in her face. The same story that I saw in my grandmothers' face when I was a child. The story of a hard life, that had survived many hardships during hard times.

Finally, I removed the picture from the wall to stack with the other photos that I intended to keep. I thought since Uncle Ray had just given me the same picture and frame, I would give this one to my sister. As I sat the picture down a strange curiosity came over me. Part of me wondered if it were possible, and part of me didn't want to know. I slowly turned the frame over. Scratched poorly on the back of the frame were the same words: *come home.*

1992

Before Misty and I left the farmhouse, we agreed not to tell Tina about the words engraved on the kitchen ceiling. She was already worried enough. Something was going on here, but I still did not understand what. There was no point in scaring her more, with something we didn't understand.

After I helped Misty off of the porch, we returned to Tina and retrieved our buckets. "There ain't nothin in there," I assured Tina.

The entire walk back to the house I spent trying to convince Tina, and myself that what we saw had to have been an animal. "There is no way a person was in that house in the state it is in," I rationalized.

We agreed to just stay away from the house for a while to let whatever animal was hiding in there, make its way out, and move on. Tina agreed that we should do just that. I could tell that I had not distracted her from the calling. As we passed the big oak, she looked back in the direction of the farmhouse one more time. I wondered if she heard the calling again at that moment. I decided not to ask. If she didn't bring it up, then neither would I.

The next few days we spent hanging out in the hidden lair and cooling off in the creek. As time passed, I found that Tina had less and less interest in spending time at the hidden fort in the trees. I suspected it was because, from the fort, there was a clear line of vision to the farmhouse. So, on Thursday I suggested that we take a day off from building the fort and play back by the creek.

After an hour of fixing our dam and splashing in the water, I was already growing bored. I had a craving for a new experience, and I knew that there was plenty of farm left to explore; if we dared.

We had never wandered much further west on the farm than the creek. According to the adults, it was dangerous back there. In the fall the woods were filled with hunters. Granddaddy swore that the swamp was surrounded by quicksand. "If someone gets stuck in that swamp, they won't get out alone," he warned us more than once.

I sat in the creek staring at the wood line, which also indicated the edge of the swamp. As curious as we were, we had never approached the edge of the swamp because we were afraid of the quicksand Granddaddy warned us about. I was ten now, soon to be eleven, I knew I was brave enough. Even if quicksand was real, I was fast and strong enough to get out now, I knew it.

I stood up in the creek and declared, "I'm going to look in the swamp."

With that, I marched out of the creek and began crossing the field toward the wood line. Neither sister tried to stop me, or talk sense into me. I could feel them behind me. They were coming too.

I slowed my pace and became more careful the closer I got to the tree line. I could feel the ground getting softer under my feet. I probably weighed ninety-five pounds, and that was a good thirty pounds heavier than my sisters. I decided that if I started sinking past my ankles, I would turn around. It occurred to me that if the trees weren't sinking, then I probably wouldn't either.

At the edge of the wood line, I peered into the swamp trying to understand how a forest and a swamp could exist in the same place. About fifty feet into the woods, the mud suddenly turned into dark black water. It was a bright sunny day, but the swamp would not allow any light into its domain. We stood there as the minutes passed, watching and waiting, but the water did not move. I knew that there had to be some flow, or there would be no creek, and maybe even no pond. I searched for ripples in the water, but there was no sign of life.

I finally worked up the courage to enter the woods. I looked back and knew that my sisters would not venture any further than the sunlight. Inch by inch I crept forward. Before I realized it, I had sunk into the mud well past my ankles. I stopped. Something caught my attention in the distance. I wasn't sure what it was, but now I had made a more interesting discovery. I could see that there was an opening on the far end of the swamp. I could see light and dry ground.

I turned to tell my sisters but realized that I was stuck. The mud had me. I tried to pull my left foot out, then I tried my right. I couldn't budge. The good news, I thought, was that I did not appear to be sinking. The bad news, I thought, was now I heard something moving.

I was scared, but I hesitated to let my sisters know. I felt that they had a flare for the dramatic, and might go get an adult. I had been confined to the house, and yard enough for one summer. I tried to calm myself. "Hey guys, it's safe, but I'm stuck. Can you come help pull me out?" I asked as calmly as possible.

I didn't hear anything else, but I could feel something, moving in the water. I was starting to feel anxious, and I could feel my nerves trembling. Misty and Tina were not moving as quickly as I hoped they would, testing each step before they took it. I couldn't complain, I'd gotten myself into this mess, and I had been warned, but I really wished they would hurry up. "Come on, hurry up before I sink any further, it's fine," I encouraged the girls.

Whatever was in the woods, or the water was circling. I could feel it getting closer. It was sizing up its prey, deciding what to do with me, I imagined. My sisters reached me, and I reached for them. They each grabbed one of my hands and pulled as hard as they could. They pulled and they pulled until they fell down. The commotion made the predator hesitate.

While my sisters got to their feet, I tried to dig out around my own. Each scoop of mud I dipped was immediately replaced by dark water and formed more mud. My sisters grabbed my arms again, this time a little higher, and strained and grunted. My feet were suctioned to the earth. I was a part of the swamp now. I let out an unexpected scream, which startled the girls.

"Wait, just wait for a second," I said as the girls let go.

I tried to relax my entire body. I had an idea. I may have been the strongest and the fastest of us three, but it was apparent it would not do me any good in this scenario. Each second that ticked away was one more opportunity for whatever was out there.

"Listen," I said to the girls, "the more I struggle, the worse I get stuck. You guys have to just pull me out without my help."

Misty and Tina looked at each other in disbelief. You would think that I had asked them to lift an elephant. They looked as if I had asked them the impossible. "You can do it," I assured them.

They each grabbed a hold of me as I instructed, at the top of my arm, under my armpit. As they began to pull, I felt a wiggle. "It's working," I encouraged them.

They pulled again, even harder, and I became a little freer from my trap. As they reset, I could tell that they were running out of energy, and out of hope. "Just one more big pull," I begged.

Just then, it was as though the swamp came to life. A strong breeze swept over the water, birds chirped, and the leaves rustled high in the trees above us. They pulled. I came free from the mud, and we all fell to the ground.

I laid there for a second and began to laugh. Suddenly, there was a low growl, and a big splash in the water. The noise sent us running for our lives, and for the field of sunlight.

7

The Far-Side of the Wooded Swamp

2020

I'd had about enough of the farmhouse, and the trailers for one day. The sun was setting, and a nice breeze had kicked up. I grabbed a bottle of water from my rental car and mounted a modern-day expedition as an adult. I cut behind Uncle Mark's imploding trailer and did not even think about looking inside. Instead, I made a beeline for the ramshackle shed. It was falling down too, and it looked like most of the tools that had once been stored there, had disappeared. I sighed and looked over the fence towards the creek. I thought, yes, that is exactly what I need after the long day I have had.

As I made my way across the field toward the creek, I wished I had brought a book with me. In my mind, the creek was a scene out of a movie. A perfect chair made in the base of an enormous oak tree, where I could sit in the roots, and put my feet in the cool trickle of water.

The creek had less water than I recalled, considering all of the other signs of a wet spring. There was certainly no way I would fit in my tree chair any longer. I sighed, I guess some things had changed. Then I thought, no they haven't, I am the one who has changed.

I looked west towards where the woods once stood that protected the black swamp. Many of the trees were gone now, and the area was mostly wide open. A number of years back Uncle Philip decided to start an excavating business, and to practice with his new equipment, he had cleared out the wooded swamp.

The trees were gone, but the swamp remained. A lesser version of what it once was, probably due to the sun finally finding the swamp, and evaporating more of the water. I walked along the water's edge noticing how much clearer the water seemed now than I remembered. No, I was right the first time, this place had changed.

1992

We speculated widely for days about what we had experienced in the woods. Based on the roar, I believed that there was another bear. Misty argued that it would have chased us out of the woods; bears don't stop. Based on the splash, Tina believed it was an alligator. I argued that alligators don't roar. For some reason, Misty believed it was a deer. When I pressed her why she claimed that she saw the deer. We simply could not make honest sense of what had happened.

We still went to the creek every afternoon to cool off in the small stream of water. While my sisters splashed and played, I would stare at the wooded swamp, remembering how it had tried to take me, and waiting for it to come again. I replayed the scene in my head a hundred times. Every emotion, the helplessness, the sense of feeling targeted, and being preyed upon. Then, I remembered, there was a backside of the swamp, and it provided a renewed sense of intrigue and hope.

I recalled the opening I saw, and the wonderment of the never explored land was too thrilling for me to ignore. If there was an opening back there, then there must be a way to get to it. I knew that there was no way my sisters were going back into the swamp, and to be honest, I didn't want too either.

I stood up and looked north, past where the trees and the swamp ended. It was open cow pasture. The cows weren't nearly as scary as the swamp, but there was one problem. It was Sam's pasture.

Everyone feared Sam. The cows feared Sam. The bulls feared Sam. The cowhands feared Sam. My sisters and I feared Sam. More importantly, we all respected Sam. Sam ate first. Sam decided where the herds could graze or not. Sam decided if the cows could enter the barn area with the grain bin, and the pond. Sam was the biggest and meanest bull that ever lived on Bristow Farms.

There were three easy ways to distinguish Sam from the other cattle. His sheer size set him apart. Most of the cows weighed in at just over one thousand pounds. Sam doubled that, easily. As for height, Sam was head and shoulders above the herd as well at nearly seven feet tall. Most of the herd were solid black. An occasional cow might have some patches, but they were all dark. Sam was solid white. His fur matched his huge horns as a dirty white. We could often spot a red brownish tint streak somewhere on his body, but it wasn't permanent, it would be blood. Sam was always into something. Most of the cattle, including the other bulls, were gentle by nature, and would only chase you for food. Sam was mean and had a temper to match. The worst thing you could do is run. A running target got Sam fired up.

I scanned the pasture, but couldn't see Sam. For a bull his size, that we were all aware of, he could be difficult to find. The color of his fur matched the bright Florida sun and the white sugar sand. He concealed quite well. I had made up my mind. I was going to the far side of the wooded swamp, but the question remained; how?

Sam's pasture fence ran right along the wood line. We had to make a choice, and either option was risky. We could re-enter the edge of the wooded swamp, and work our way down the wood line, which would better conceal us from Sam, but I wasn't sure if the swamp monster was much better. If we crossed the fence into the pasture, we would have a more open path, and feel safer from the swamp, unless Sam spotted us. I made the pitch to my sisters.

"Why do we have to go back there?" Misty asked in a whiney voice.

"I told you, it looks amazing, aren't you interested to know what exactly is back there?" I tried to hook her.

Tina chimed in, "not if it means getting eaten or gored."

"We won't, I promise. Either way we go, we will go low and slow," I assured the girls, "and safely," I added for emphasis.

Neither of the girls looked interested at all. "Ok, if you vote to cut through the edge of the swamp, raise your hand."

I half raised my hand to encourage them. Neither made a move. I hesitated a second. Let them think for a minute I thought. "Ok, then who votes to cut down the side of Sam's pen?"

I shot my hand up as high as I could. Misty and Tina looked to one another but did not otherwise move immediately. Finally, Misty half-heartedly raised her hand, a little. Yes, Tina was defeated again. "I am going to the fence line to look down, and try to scout where we need to go and look for Sam," I told the girls, "come on whenever you're ready."

I looked as far as I could down the fence line, but could not see the end of the fence, or the tree line. I focused my efforts on locating Sam. It was a large pasture, at least forty acres, and there were plenty of hiding spots under enormous shade trees. I spotted some cows laying under the trees, and a few grazing in the field, but I could not see Sam.

My sisters joined me a few minutes later, and I shared my plan. "We are going to cross the fence down there by the trees, and then walk slowly down the fence line until it opens up on the other side, then we can cross," I instructed.

Tina piped up finally, "I think that we should run."

Misty corrected her sister before I could, "are you crazy?! If Sam sees us running, we are all goners."

Misty wasn't wrong, I thought. "No matter what, do not run unless absolutely necessary. Don't expect the fence to save us from Sam. If he is running and has a target, the fence will not even slow him down. If it comes to that, and you make it across the fence, keep going. Don't stop, and don't look back. Just run to the shed."

The girls nodded that they understood the seriousness of my orders. Moments later, we were walking in Sam's pasture for the first time ever.

The sun was behind the trees, which in turn cast shade on us. I hoped that it would serve as concealment too. We walked slightly slower than at a normal pace. Scanning the field, and then scanning the wood line. Everything was peaceful.

The opening wasn't nearly as far as I was expecting, maybe only a quarter of a mile. As we crossed back over the fence, I sighed in relief. Adults make everything seem worse than they really are, not kids.

A couple of hundred feet from the fence I could see water. As we approached it, I realized that there did not appear to be any oak trees in this area. Instead, there were dozens of pine trees, and they were spread out nicely, with plenty of room in between, which allowed the perfect amount of sunlight. As we got closer, I expected the ground to become soft and muddy, but it did not. I tried to force all of my weight downward into the earth, but it was firm.

My sisters were the first to notice it, probably because I was still quite wary of danger. "It's a beach!" Tina announced joyously.

I looked in the direction that they were now running, and sure enough, there appeared to be a large area of white sand. I joined my sisters to investigate. They were already sitting in the wet sand, building sandcastles. Where were we, I wondered. I stepped around the girls and made my way to the water's edge. The ground held firm. There was a nice size pool of water. The water was draining toward the swamp, but slow enough that an area, of maybe twelve feet, had built, and filled in. It looked like the water was two or three feet deep. The most surprising find was that the water was not black and murky like the swamp, and pond water. It was colored like the creek, a light red, but appeared clearer because the ground under the water was white.

I laughed aloud, and turned back to my sisters, "I told you it would be worth it," I shouted, then turned around, and jumped into the pool of red water.

The girls joined me for a grand time. We splashed and floated on top of the water. This was way better than the shallow creek. It may have been the most fun that we had the entire summer. Pure, innocent, child play. It also may have been the last time I remember us ever having that kind of fun together.

After about thirty minutes of water play, I was feeling waterlogged. I realized that there was still much to explore in our new-found paradise. I climbed out of the water hole and continued my expedition. Instead of walking further west, I decided to move back toward the wooded swamp, and see what it looked like from this side.

Rather than an abrupt line of trees in a field, which is how the other side suddenly appeared, this side developed more gradually. The closer I moved to the swamp, the thicker the brush, and the trees became. I noticed the ground was getting soft, and muddy again, and did my best to stay on firm ground.

I was close enough now that I could smell the swamp water. I took a big leap to intentionally step onto a limb that I spotted and assumed would not sink. When I landed on it, the limb broke and made a loud snap. Suddenly a rafter of turkeys took off, seemingly out of nowhere, and scared the bejeezus out of me. Six or seven turkeys fluttered off to the west gobbling all the way.

The ruckus alerted my sisters, and they ran over to me still overwhelmed by the fun that we had found. We were turned with our backs to the swamp watching the turkeys try to fly away completely oblivious to any danger that may have existed on the west side of the wooded swamp. Tina pointed, "what is that?"

I looked to Tina who had turned back towards the swamp and was pointing to something on the ground. I couldn't tell what it was from our position, but it was in the area that the turkeys had come from. I moved carefully toward the object uncertain of what to expect. It wasn't moving. As I got closer, I realized it was not one object, but many. They were sprawled out of an area of ten or fifteen feet.

My sisters were right behind me, and they realized what it was at the same time I did. "They're bones," Misty spoke first.

Tina asked, "from what?"

I added, "or who?"

There were dozens if not hundreds of bones piled up, and spread out in this drier, but still savannah-like area. The white sand was mixed with the dark mud here, and there were sporadic bunches of tall grass. To the north was relatively open, but to the south was nothing but thicket, and to the east, the swamp sat silently only fifty feet away.

We kicked the bones around shuffling the scene for a moment in silence. Taking in what we had found. Trying to understand it. Many of the bones were large, and I assumed that they were cow bones, but why were they there? Other bones were smaller, and for some reason, those were creepier to me. Tina broke the silence with an observation I least expected.

"You know how Grandma told us that the creek was red because of the acid in the leaves?" I couldn't tell if she was making a statement or asking a question.

Unsure what the creek had to do with the bones, I was tempted to ignore her. Misty took the bait, "yeah, what about it?"

"Well that water over there that we were just swimming in, must come from the ground, and the sand is white, but I don't see any leaves. So, why is the water red?" she begged for someone to kill the idea which had entered her young mind.

I didn't understand what she was inferring at first, and I could tell that Misty was contemplating her question too. I bent down and picked up a long bone so that I could inspect it more closely. It had obviously been there for a long time and had long since been picked clean by woodland creatures. I held it up so that I could see the bone, and the waterhole at the same time. "You think the water is red because of this?" I asked sarcastically.

There were a lot of bones, but I suspected it would take much more to color a water source. One thing was for certain, something strange was going on back here. No, I thought, something strange is going on back here and at the farmhouse. Or maybe it was really the pond that created the calling. Perhaps it was all tied to the red water that came from the white ground, next to a pile of bones. Something strange was happening at Bristow Farms.

The girls had picked up bones of their own now and were playing.

Misty had found a large cow cranium, and it looked like they were trying to put the cow back together again. I couldn't shake the thought that something was wrong. "Well, unless we want to become a part of this pile, I suggest that we…" I was interrupted by a large splash.

"That wasn't no bullfrog," I shouted.

We all ran just as fast as our little legs would take us. Huffing and puffing we reached the fence line faster than I thought we could. Now we had a dilemma. Run with the bull, or make do with the monster. It would be nearly impossible to run through the edge of the wood line on the other side of the fence. It was completely overgrown. We would have to take our chances with Sam.

As I held the barbed wire for my sisters to cross, I scanned the field for Sam. Still no sign of him, good. We bolted down the fence line. The girls were scared to tears, and I wasn't far behind them. Then, from the corner of my eye, I saw Sam. He saw me too, and he was charging.

It seems an unnatural thing for cattle to run, but when they do it is a wonder to behold. Over two thousand pounds of bone, and muscle. An unstoppable force. I shouted to my sisters, "Sam! Go into the woods, I will distract him," I commanded.

They understood my guidance as they peeled off and dove under the fence. I continued running, but now I did everything I could to make sure that I had Sam's attention. I jumped as high as I could, and waved my arms and hollered, "Hey Sam, you suck!"

It worked. He was locked onto me and gaining ground quickly. I was literally running for my life. It is hard to run as fast as you can while looking for a tree to jump into. Any escape was all I could hope for. I could see the opening on the other side of the fence ahead. From there it was another five hundred feet to the shed. I hoped if I could make it that far, I could hide inside, confuse the bull, and he might leave.

I started working out how to get on the other side of the fence the quickest way possible. Rolling on the ground, under the fence as my sisters had done, in cow manure was not particularly appealing to me. Up ahead I noticed a section of the wire was loose and hanging. That was my exit. I was going to jump over the fence.

A ten-year-old kid jumping over a fence isn't as unbelievable as it sounds. The wire was strung at four feet high, but this piece was sagging at least a foot. I jumped over the same sag by the garden a hundred times before. It was all about the timing.

I launched into the air, and sprung over the wire, almost. My left foot snagged on a barb, and I tumbled to the other side. While jumping up, I spotted Sam thirty yards away and closing. It was clear that I was not going to make it to the shed. I had another idea.

There was a farm gate installed fifty feet further down. I sprinted to it, and collapsed on the ground. As if I were dead. If I were wrong, I probably would be dead. Sam hit the brakes at the gate, which appeared much sturdier than the rickety fence. He stood staring at me huffing for what seemed like a long time. I dared not move a muscle, but I could not stop breathing heavily, and I was sure that my heart was about to beat out of my chest. The great thing about large herbivores is that, even if they are mad, they are not trying to eat you. As such, there was no incentive to stay. Sam slowly walked away grazing on his grass as if nothing had just happened.

I laid still for at least five minutes after Sam turned away. I wanted to give him time to forget me. Finally, I sat up. Sam paid no attention to me; I was no longer his concern. I looked to the wooded swamp. There was no sign of my sisters, and I was sure that they were right where I had left them. The question was, how in the world would they get out now.

I walked to the corner where the woods met the fence to think, keeping an eye on Sam the entire time. He was just interested enough not to wander too far. As I reached the corner, Misty emerged from the wood line about one hundred feet from the fence.

"What the heck, are you crazy?" I asked incredulously as I made my way down to her.

By the time I reached her, she was on the ground sobbing. It was then that I realized that our baby sister was missing. "Where is Tina?" I asked.

Misty looked up at me with tears in her eyes. Then she looked back into the woods. I expected the worst, but Misty just said, "I don't know, she was right behind me, and then she wasn't."

"You left her?!" I chided.

"No, she was behind me, and then it got sticky, so she tried a different path. She was ahead of me the last time I saw her. It's so thick in there," Misty was sobbing again, and not making any sense.

I noticed now that Misty's arms, and legs were bleeding badly. It seemed silly to ask, "are you hurt?"

For the first time, I think, she looked at her cuts and abrasions. Despite how she looked and knowing that she must be in pain, she responded, "No, I'm fine."

I sighed, "Ok, you stay right here. I am going to go look for Tina."

I started to enter the brush, then I turned back to Misty, "if I'm not back in twenty minutes, you had better go get someone."

That simple yet obvious statement implied the seriousness of the situation. We always relied on ourselves to solve our problems. Going to our grandparents would only be an absolute last resort. We knew it would likely mean the end of our summer and our freedom.

I stopped just inside of the wood line and shouted, "Tina, can you hear me?"

There was no response, and for a moment I considered calling in the cavalry. Instead, I grit my teeth and plowed into the unknown. There was no relief in the thicket. No clearings at all. Just one bush of thorns after another. The only good news was that it appeared to be fairly dry, and mud-free.

As if someone had read my thoughts, there was a loud low rumble of thunder in the distance. It shouldn't have been a surprise on a midafternoon summer day in Florida, but it was disheartening nonetheless. The thunder sounded far off, but storms move swiftly this time of year, and I fully expected a downpour within minutes. I had to move quickly, but also carefully.

Once I was well into the woods, I called out for Tina again, although I didn't really expect a response. However, I thought that I might have heard something so I called again, "Tina, can you hear me?"

I listened closely for anything. I heard a soft response, "help me."

I couldn't tell if she was far away, or whispering. I tried to speed up. It was impossible. The routine had to be, take a step, free myself from the thicket, then take another step. I called Tina again, but this time with guidance, "Tina, yell HELP every thirty seconds so I can find you."

I stood still for a moment until she complied. Her voice was too far to tell where the sound was coming from. It was as though it was both reverberating from every tree in the woods, and yet being dampened by them at the same time. My only course of action was to keep moving forward. I knew that soon Tina's voice would also be competing with a storm, and that motivated me to hurry.

After five more minutes of fighting weeds, I felt like I had a sense of which direction Tina might be in. I needed to stop heading west, toward the far-side, and start heading south, toward the swamp. The realization made my stomach turn.

I knew I was getting closer to my sister, but her voice was also getting fainter. My imagination ran wild with what might be happening to her. Maybe she was sinking in the swamp. Maybe she was being eaten by something. I started crying at the thought of losing my sister. I wiped the tears from my cheek and realized that all I had managed to do was replace the tears with blood. Then I started thinking about how blood attracted many predators. I needed to push it all out of my mind and find my damn sister.

It did not take long to realize that I was definitely on the right track. I was close now. It had begun to sprinkle, or perhaps more, it was hard to tell under the protection of the thick canopy. I had a feeling that I was no more than ten feet away from Tina, but I just could not see her. The ground was getting soft, but for the most part, it was holding. If it was holding me, it was holding my sister, I rationalized.

Finally, I spotted her bright red hair. I had always told her that she should feel blessed to have her colored hair. Misty's and my own hair were so typical and boring I told her. She was crumpled over on the ground in the middle of the biggest thicket I had seen yet. The thicket had thorns that were big as pocket knife blades.

I told Tina that I could see her. I expected her to jump up. She did not. "I'm gonna get you out, just stay where you are," I tried to assure her.

If I had taken the time to think I would have gotten a machete from the shed. She was somehow embedded into the thicket. She looked as though the thick vines of thorns were growing out of her. I couldn't understand how she had gotten so terribly tangled. It would take forever to get her out.

It was raining hard now, and Tina could not help at all. If it weren't for her whimpering, I would have thought that she was unconscious. I imagined having dozens of knife blades bearing down on her, some likely stuck in her. I could not break most of the vines, only move them. To move them took great care.

I took what felt like hours to finally reach Tina. I kept expecting to hear Mark, or Granddaddy cutting through the woods coming to the rescue. I was relieved once I unsnagged Tina, and realized she could walk. I don't think it would have been possible to carry her out of that mess. She limped along beside me as we backtracked our way out of the wooded swamp. She never said a word, until we were safely out.

I was shocked when we returned to the field to find Misty sitting right where I left her in the pouring rain. I couldn't believe that she didn't go for help, as I had told her. She must have seen the surprise on my face because the first thing she said was, "I went to the house for help, but no one was there."

The rain was slacking off, and none of us were in a huge hurry to get home. I had no idea how we would explain all of the cuts. Now that we were free, I felt the need to ask Tina again, "are you ok?"

She had been trembling nonstop since I had found her, and it only seemed to be getting worse. I didn't know if it was nerves, or if she was cold from the rain. Probably a mix of both. She responded to us so softly that I could barely make out what she was saying, "I saw it."

"What did you say," I leaned in so I could hear her better.

"I said, I saw it," she reiterated.

"You saw what?" Misty put her arm around Tina.

Tina paused, "I saw the monster."

"The monster?" I exclaimed, confused.

It took me a second to realize what she meant, "oh, was it a bear?" I asked.

She nodded her head no.

"Was it an alligator?" Misty asked.

She nodded her head no again.

We all stood silent for a minute. I think the poor girl was probably in shock and confused. Instead of questioning her further about it, I said, "ok, well we are safe now. Let's go home, and get cleaned up before anyone gets back, and we might just survive tonight too."

2020

It got late quicker than I expected. The sun had all but set, and twilight had brought the mosquitos. I headed back to the house. Because I had expected the trailer to be disgusting, I also brought a tent. I decided I would camp in the front yard tonight, and build a nice campfire.

When I finished setting up my tent, I checked my phone for the first time since arriving. That was the best part about the farm; weak signal. It was easy to cut off from the rest of the word. Neither cable nor internet had made its way out to Bristow Farms by 2020 unless you had a satellite, there were no fiber optics. I doubted there ever would be.

To my surprise, I had received several texts, all of which I had no way to respond too. The only text that interested me at all was from my cousin John that read: *Daddy told me you are at the farm. Brent and I will grab some beer, and be out that way in a bit.*

As much as I had looked forward to some alone time on the farm, the company was a welcomed surprise. Maybe I'd had enough alone time for one day. I felt like I was remembering too much too fast.

Just as I got the fire roaring, I saw Johns' Ram headlights bouncing across the field. I didn't get back to Hawthorne often enough, but I could always count on John and Brent making time to see me. We sat around the fire until after midnight drinking beers and telling lies about the good ol days. Sharing conquests, and stories of other classmates and friends.

It wasn't until we had just about run out of beer, and other things to talk about that John asked, "How are Misty and Tina?"

A large gust of wind swept in from the north, and tried to kill the fire, but ended up only strengthening it. I took the last chug of my beer and threw the can into the fire. "Well, Tina is somewhere local around here, but she won't come out to the farm. Misty lives out in New Mexico, and she wonders if even that is far enough away."

The air fell silent until John finally said, "yeah, that was pretty screwed up what happened."

8

She's Still Here

1992

We got home, cleaned up, and changed before my grandparents got home. There would still be a reckoning when Grandma washed our clothes and saw them all tore up, but at least we would survive today. The rest of the evening was uncharacteristically low key. I don't think any of us said anything to one another. We watched a little television, and all went to bed early. Our grandparents didn't question or complain.

The next morning, I was up at the break of dawn. Normally my Granddaddy woke me up on his way out of the door to work so that I could get started with my own chores. I figured I woke up early because I went to bed early. As I was finishing breakfast, Misty emerged from the girl's bedroom groggy-eyed. "Good morning sunshine," I laughed.

Misty stumbled into the bathroom the same time that Granddaddy walked out the front door for work. Grandma was getting ready to leave herself. Misty grabbed a bowl and a spoon and joined me at the breakfast table for a bowl of cereal. It was obvious that she had not slept well, and I could not resist poking fun at her. "May I just say, that you look lovely this morning," I laughed at my own silliness.

Misty did not laugh. Her hair was tossed and tangled, she had drool marks on her face, and her eyes were dark as though she had not slept in a week. "Tina kept me awake half of the night, whimpering and crying," she scowled.

That thought saddened me enough to stop picking on Misty. "Well, at least she is sleeping in then," I observed.

"What do you mean?" asked Misty with honest confusion.

I just looked at her as though she must be dreaming with her eyes open. Before I could make a snide remark about Tina not being at the table, Misty got up and looked around the wood-paneled wall that split the double-wide trailer, into the living room. When she turned back to me, her face was full of surprise. "Tina is not in bed, have you seen her?"

Shocked myself, I shook my head no. I got up from the table, dropped my bowl and spoon in the sink, and then poked my head into the girl's room. Misty wasn't kidding, Tina was not in bed. I returned to the table, "Eat your breakfast, I will go look outside."

I started out the door, but then stopped, and turned back to Misty, "don't tell Grandma," I instructed.

I checked the front, then I checked the back. There was no sign of Tina, but I couldn't call for her while Grandma was still home. As I returned from the back yard, I saw Grandma loading into the van. I waved to her goodbye, and she responded with reminders of several things she wanted me to get done while she was gone.

As soon as the van pulled onto washed-out road, I called for Tina. For a ten-year-old, my voice carried very well, and I knew that Tina should be able to hear me from almost anywhere she could be this time of morning. Misty heard me from inside and joined me. I realized that she had taken the time to at least brush her hair.

"She isn't anywhere around the trailer," I apprised Misty.

"Why would she be outside so early in the morning," Misty asked me the same question that I had been pondering.

"Are we sure that she isn't in the house?" I realized.

I sent Misty back inside to search the house for her, while I continued calling outside. I didn't expand my search because I was fairly certain that Misty would find her curled up sleeping, probably in the back room. The backroom was where Granddaddy slept. It was the only room in the house with air conditioning. It had a small window unit which he would turn on an hour before bedtime. By an hour after he had fallen asleep, the room turned into an icebox. My Grandma refused to sleep back there because it was too cold. Sometimes, if the heat were just unbearable, us kids would make pallets on the floor, and sleep in the back room too. More often, after Granddaddy got up to leave for work in the morning, we would take over the cool room for another hour, or two of sleep, if we could.

Misty returned a few minutes later shrugging her shoulders, "she isn't in the house."

Now I was getting mad. What was she thinking, taking off this early in the morning without telling anyone? I told Misty to stay around the house in case Tina turned up. I was going to look for her.

I started with the obvious spots. First, I checked the forts. Then I checked the shed, the old trailer in the woods, the camper, and even Mark's house. I spotted Aunt Tojuanna mowing her yard, and so I ran up to her and asked, "have you seen Tina?"

She cut off the mower. "I sure haven't. Is she missing?" I feared that she sensed that something was wrong.

"No ma'am, we are playing hide-and-seek," I was quick on my toes.

"Ok, you kids be careful and have fun. Holler if you need anything," she said as she cranked the lawnmower back up.

I ran back to the trailer. Tina had not returned on her own. It was 8:30 now, the sun was well into the sky, and I knew that she should be awake, wherever she was. I stood in the front yard scanning the horizon, looking for some indication of where my sister might be. I realized that I hadn't checked the creek or the barn. It was a long shot, but what other options were there.

I started with the creek. My gut told me that it was too early, and cool for her to be in the water, and thankfully, I was right. I made my way around to the barn. The barnyard was filled with cattle who were eyeing me, waiting for me to enter so that they could rush to me for food. I saw Uncle Philip working in the barn. That was a pretty good indicator to me, that Tina was not in there. I continued around the perimeter to the other side until I reached the road which would take me back by the big oak, and on to the trailer.

I glanced back toward the barn one last time, but something else caught my attention. There was something on the front porch of the old farmhouse that I did not remember from the other day. As I got closer, I realized it was Tina's blanket. Tina's blanket was reversible cotton and was green on one side, and white on the other. I pulled the blanket off of the porch trying to make sense of why it was there. Suddenly, I heard movement inside of the house. I jumped back in surprise. Then, I began piecing things together. I crept back toward the porch and peeked inside the open-door frame. I spotted something red lying on the floor. It only took me a split second to realize it was Tina.

Without hesitation, I jumped up onto the porch and called out to Tina. Before I could make it to the doorway, she sat up, looked directly at me, and said, "good morning," as if this were the most normal thing to ever happen.

Tina rose to her feet and met me at the door. I was both confused and furious. "Are you ok?" I asked with genuine concern.

She simply responded, "yes," and did not offer anymore.

Trying to contain my outrage I continued, "what are you doing here?"

Tina looked at me as though I might have lost my mind, "I couldn't sleep," she responded.

"What?!" now I could no longer hold my anger.

"We have been looking for you all morning! You can't just disappear, and not tell anyone where you are going," I berated her.

With no emotion, Tina simply responded, "I'm sorry."

I let out a loud frustrated sigh. "Come on, let's go," I instructed her.

I picked up her blanket, then helped her down from the porch. As we slowly made our way back to the trailer, I had time to think. "Why did you go to the old farmhouse?" I asked Tina.

"I told you, because I couldn't sleep," she immediately responded as if scripted.

Her answer still did not make sense to me. "Why couldn't you sleep?" I asked.

"Because I was scared," she answered.

"If you are scared of the farmhouse, then why would you go to it," I asked, then added, "alone."

"I'm not scared of the farmhouse," Tina replied clearly.

Now I was confused even more. Her words made sense, but they were an abrupt change from recent events. Obviously, she wasn't scared of the house anymore if she were sleeping in it alone, but what had changed? "Well then, what were you scared of?" I begged.

Tina responded to me as if she were pleading with me to believe her, "I am scared of the monster."

Nothing that had happened that morning made any sense to me. When we reached the trailer, we basically rehashed the exact conversation with Misty. Misty was visibly as confused as I was, but she was not nearly as willing to try to understand. The frustration from a night of poor sleep I assumed.

The rest of the day was fairly uneventful. No one was in the mood for an adventure. We completed our chores and played in the yard until our grandparents got home. Then we worked in the garden, had family dinner, snapped some green beans while watching Seinfeld on NBC, and headed to bed.

Misty was asleep by nine o'clock. I woke her up enough to lead her to bed and watched her zonk back out. Grandma put Tina to bed, and then came into my room to tuck me in. Grandma brought a new *Detective Zach* book with her. Occasionally, she would read with me a bit before bed, and I appreciated it because it was our only real personal bonding time, and it felt special.

I slept deeply that night. I did not wake up before my grandfather the next morning. As a matter of fact, he tried to wake me up, but I never made it out of bed. Grandma woke me up again before she left,

"Don't sleep all day. Get up, and wake the girls up when you do," she instructed.

With those words of guidance, she left for the day. A few minutes later I drug myself out of bed, and to the toilet. As I exited the bathroom, I opened the girl's door across the hallway, turned on the light, and shouted, "rise and shine!" as obnoxiously as possible.

Misty threw a pillow at me, but I dodged it and laughed at her. I looked at Tina's bed. It was empty. "You have got to be kidding me!" I exclaimed loudly as Misty looked up to see what about.

There was no extensive search this morning. We knew right where to go. This time Misty joined me, and we planned to have a 'come to Jesus' conversation with our baby sister.

We could see Tina on the floor in the farmhouse before we even entered. Again, her blanket was on the front porch, and she was curled up on the floor in the kitchen. I asked Misty rhetorically, "why doesn't she have her blanket on? Why carry it all the way here, then leave it on the porch?"

I motioned to Misty to keep quiet as we entered the house. Something was going on here, and I hoped perhaps there might be a clue. We watched Tina sleeping on the floor for several minutes as we also searched the house from the doorway. Everything seemed as it had always been, cluttered and useless.

When I was satisfied that there was nothing to learn, I bent down and shook Tina awake. She immediately got up looking as refreshed as I had ever seen her. Like she had slept better than she had all summer. I was just looking at Tina, trying to understand, when Misty spoke first, "What are you doing?"

Again, Tina responded as though this were perfectly normal, "I was sleeping."

"Tina, we just agreed yesterday that you would not come up here without telling us," I reminded her.

"She said I shouldn't wake you, that you needed the sleep," Tina responded.

I looked to Misty who was refuting Tina's excuse by shaking her head no, "I did not!" Misty said.

Tina clarified, "not you, the lady."

I had enough, "Tina, there is no lady!"

Tina calmly responded, "yes, there is."

"I thought you were afraid of her. I thought that you hated this house," Misty pointed out to Tina.

Tina was silent for a second, then responded, "that was because I didn't understand that she is trying to protect me."

"From the monster," I sarcastically added.

"Yes," was all Tina said.

"An invisible woman is protecting you from an invisible monster?" I hoped that she would understand how she sounded.

Without raising her voice, or showing any emotion, she simply said, "yes."

I grabbed her arm and pulled her from the house. I was done being gentle with her. I basically pushed her off of the porch, and shouted, "well you can tell her that I will protect you because you are not allowed to come to this house anymore, or I will tell Grandma!"

Suddenly, the entire house rattled, and the few remaining windows shook until the glass broke. Misty and I jumped down and joined Tina who did not seem bothered at all by the event. We stood there for a long time, watching the house. Waiting for something else to happen. I finally turned to Tina and said, "Tina, you must understand, you cannot go back into that house."

Tina made no indication that she heard me, or accepted my wisdom. We all walked back to the trailer in silence. Not much was said that day. We didn't play together. As a matter of fact, I cannot recall anything else happening that day. It was as if we did not exist to one another. Eventually, the sun set, and we all went to bed.

I could not sleep. Correction, I would not sleep. I sat on the floor, quietly at my door which I kept cracked, watching my sister's closed door. The hours ticked by, and I struggled to keep my eyes open. I began nodding off when suddenly, I would shake myself awake. I checked my

O.D. Green Timex watch. It was two a.m. when the door opened, and Tina left the room.

She had her blanket wrapped around her shoulders, and it appeared to me that she was not sleep walking, she was awake. She stopped in the kitchen and opened either a drawer, or a cabinet. Then she made her way out of the front door, taking care not to make any more noise than absolutely necessary. It was all quite intentional.

I waited inside until I figured she was out of the yard, and would not notice me following her. Then I slipped out and used the cover of darkness to follow my youngest sister sneaking out, to another house, during the middle of the night. The entire scenario was senseless to me.

Sure enough, she walked directly, and purposefully to the farmhouse. She climbed up onto the porch of the dilapidated building, and there she stopped. She took off her blanket, and carefully folded it up, and placed it on the porch. Then she entered the house.

I expected her to immediately lay down, and go to sleep. I wasn't sure what my plan was, but I had a sense that something else would happen. I was hiding behind a bale of hay and was unable to see Tina once she entered the house. The house somehow seemed even creepier at night. I felt as though someone was watching me. I was about to approach the farmhouse when it appeared that a light came on.

I thought to myself that perhaps that is what she retrieved from the kitchen, a flashlight. When I noticed the light move, I realized that it wasn't a flashlight at all. As plain as day, I could see a lady standing over Tina who was laying on the floor.

The lady was wearing a full-length white nightgown which covered her entire body from her feet to her neck. From where I stood, she appeared to be young, and beautiful. It seemed as though there was something familiar about her. The most shocking feature was, she appeared to be glowing. It was her essence that was lighting the house.

Tina sat up. They appeared to be talking to one another. Then, completely unexpectedly, Tina turned in my direction, as if she knew I was there. As if she had been told I was there. I quickly slipped back behind the bale of hay and dropped to the ground. I was scared frozen.

I sat for a minute considering my options. Maybe I should just go home, and forget what I saw. I knew where Tina was. I could come get her in the morning. However, I was worried about Tina. She seemed safe for the moment, but what was happening here was not natural. She could not just sleep here every night. Soon the summer would be over, and school would start. After that, winter would come. Why did she leave the blanket on the porch I wondered?

I peeked back around the corner of the bale of hay. The light was out. The lady was gone. Where was Tina? Sleeping on the floor I assumed. I had to make a decision: leave her, or go and get her.

I stood up slowly, and silently. As I emerged from the bale of hay, I expected the light to come back on, and the lady to reappear. When neither happened, I began to move toward the house. I had never been more frightened in my entire life. I strained through the dark to try and see Tina. I could not see inside of the house at all. It was as if it had somehow been blackened, and devoid of all light. I couldn't help but notice the moonlight reflecting from the pond. It was a clear night, and there was plenty of natural light, I should be able to see inside of the house, I thought.

I reached the porch, but I still could not see or hear Tina inside of the house. I was too afraid to enter. I called out, "Tina, are you in there?"

I was answered by complete silence. Even the crickets seem to stop chirping. "Tina," I begged, "come on, stop fooling about. It's time to come home."

Again, there was no response. I climbed onto the porch next to Tina's' blanket. I still could not see into the house, but I could feel a presence. I wondered if it were Tina's, or the spirits. I tried to convince myself that it was just Tina, and I needed to get my sister out of there.

I stepped into the doorway, into complete darkness, and announced myself one last time, "Tina, you need to come home," I pleaded.

Before I could say anymore or react, Tina appeared right in front of me in the doorway. The house was suddenly lit by the spirit which stood directly behind Tina, not more than three feet away from me.

Finally, Tina spoke to say, "I am home."

A coldness fell over me. I could not move. I could not speak. I stumbled back out of the doorway onto the porch. Something ached in my gut. I looked down. Sticking out of my stomach, was a familiar butcher knife.

2020

I woke up the next morning feeling like I had drunk all of the beer in Hawthorne. My head was pounding, and I dared not open my eyes, lest I risk literal death. My stomach hurt. It was not the normal morning after drinking way too much sickness, but more of a stinging pain. I rubbed my belly and felt an old scar that reminded me where I was.

I could tell that I had not made it into my tent last night, and was covered in dew. Surprisingly, I was not very cold. I must have brought my sleeping bag out by the fire in my drunken wisdom. I didn't remember any of it. I didn't even remember saying goodbye to John and Brent, or them leaving. Perhaps they were still here too I thought. I wasn't ready to pull the hat from my eyes to find out. Just lay here for a few more minutes, then I will assess the damage I thought.

"Boy, ya'll must have tied one on last night," I heard a familiar voice.

All of the Bristow's have a distinctive sound, almost as if they spoke their own dialect. "I saw that ya'll had a big fire going up there, but I figured that I would just catch up with ya today," he said.

I could now tell that the person talking to me was my Uncle Philip. Philip had run the bulk of the farm his entire life. Almost all of the cattle, the farm equipment, and the acreage belonged to him. He was getting older now, and finding it more difficult to run a ranch. Ranching is a young man's game; he would always say.

I needed to get up to greet my uncle, and I didn't mean to be rude, but it was hard. As I was forcing myself to rise, I realized what he had just said, 'fire going up there.' Confused, I opened my eyes and took my hat off. The sun blinded me, and it took me a few seconds to adjust. I looked back to see Philip leaning against his truck. Then, I looked down, my heart stopped beating, and I lost my breath.

I had awakened under the big pecan tree. Right where the front porch to the old farmhouse used to sit. I was covered by Tina's childhood blanket.

9

One's Ending is Another's Beginning

The next morning, on his way to the barn to tend to the cows, Uncle Philip found me sprawled out under the big pecan tree in front of the old farmhouse. Tina's blanket was tied around my abdomen, serving as a makeshift tourniquet. I had nearly bled out by the time the ambulance arrived, but Tina's blanket was saving my life.

I was rushed to Shand's Hospital, which was forty minutes away, the next town over. Most of the nursing staff and young doctors consisted of students from the University of Florida, who were not accustomed to seeing young children with this kind of injury. As they learned the story, that I had nearly been murdered by my eight-year-old sister, shock and sympathy overwhelmed my care team.

The incident even made the Gainesville-Sun, which was the major newspaper in the region. Of course, there was wild speculation, but nothing was mentioned about a spirit or a strange lady. Instead, the article focused on a life that doesn't exist anymore. It told the story of children left home alone, exploring the wilderness, the work we did, and of course then the stabbing.

When the police came to talk to me, I had no other choice, I had to tell them that Tina had stabbed me. There was simply no other way to fix what had happened, I believed. They appeared to already know before I answered. The police seemed more concerned with why she had stabbed me, than the actual stabbing.

I knew that I couldn't mention the spirit. They would lock me up in a padded cell next to Tina. I told them everything that happened right up until the night of the incident. I told them about Tina falling off of the raft in the pond, and about her being lost in the wooded-swamp. When they asked me about a monster, I realized they must have already questioned my sisters. I concurred that Tina was nearly attacked by some sort of animal, but I didn't know what exactly.

I was in the hospital for more than three weeks. I spent my eleventh birthday in surgery. That was my fourth, and final operation. My Grandma stayed with me most of the time for the first week, but then she had to go back to work. She still came to see me every day when she finished her cleaning. She never once mentioned Tina.

I half expected to be in some sort of trouble. I at least thought that my grandparents would be mad at me. That didn't seem to be the case at all. They actually appeared to be sorry, but I wasn't sure what for. Then I realized that they had their own trouble with the authorities. Apparently, our way of life did not make sense or sit well with city folk.

I never saw Tina at the hospital, but I didn't expect to. Misty came once or twice, but we didn't speak. She was just in the room. I caught her looking at me, and we made momentary eye contact. Her big brown eyes looked even more doe-like than ever. She kept her head down after that, and I couldn't help but wonder what she thought about all of this.

I was finally allowed to go home on July 30th. When I got there, I had been warned that Tina was gone. The state had hauled her off for psychiatric evaluation, and rehabilitation. She had left the day that I was taken to the hospital. We did not know if, or when she might return.

My summer was over. All I could do was rest, and heal. My worst nightmare was being stuck in the hotbox all day, during the dead of summer, but there was some good news. We wouldn't be staying in the hotbox. We had to go to work with Grandma. Our days of being left alone on the farm were over.

Grandma was a maid for three different rich families. She cleaned one of their houses every day of the week. All three of the houses had pools. That was great news for Misty. She would get to swim every day. It was torture for me. I couldn't swim because of my injuries. At least I would be in the air conditioning and would have cable t.v. to get me through the days. Maybe this tragedy wasn't the end of the world after all.

Tina returned just before school started back. The psychiatrist had cleared her to return to the family and declared it was essential to her recovery that she start back to school with her siblings. He said that the attack was an isolated incident, induced by stressful life-threatening events. He believed that the pond and the woods had temporarily altered Tina's psyche, making her believe that she was in constant danger. In his final report, he described Tina as a perfectly normal little girl with a bright future. I hoped that was true.

Maybe the experts were right. Maybe it was all my fault, although they didn't say so directly. I forced Tina onto the raft. I made the girls explore the wooded swamp with me. Maybe it was my own fault that Tina had stabbed me. I was more worried about what I might have done to Tina, than what she had done to me.

The reunion was staged by her psychiatrist. He would bring her out to the farm, and Misty and Grandma would meet them outside. Then, they would bring Tina inside to make a formal apology to me. He said that it was a necessary part of her healing process. To me, it felt weird and fake. When Tina entered the front door, I was supposed to be sitting on the couch. I did not want her to think that I was in pain, so I stood instead. As soon as the door closed, I didn't wait, I walked right up to Tina, and gave her a hug, to show her I was fine, and that there was no ill will between us.

She immediately began sobbing. She kept saying over and over that she didn't mean to. I believe that was true. I told her that I knew, and it would all be ok. I hoped that was true too.

The next week school began, and we all got busy. Everyone in school had heard different versions of what happened. I was asked constantly for the truth. I refused to say anything about the incident. I was worried about what it might do to Tina. Thankfully, not many eight-year old's read the newspaper.

Our expeditions had ended. Not because of what had happened so much, but because there was little time for it during the school year. The first day that we had free was a Sunday, and I was back to my regular self. There was a sense of hesitation, but in the end, we decided to check on the hidden lair.

Things felt like they were before; after an hour or so. All was forgotten, and we had no worries. We did some building, we did some playing, and then we did some relaxing. No one had said a word in fifteen minutes. We were all enjoying the breeze on our respective branches. Out of nowhere Misty looked at me and asked, "why?"

"Why what?" I asked right back.

Misty looked confused, "why should we go home?"

"Uh, I dunno," I responded.

"Well then, why did you say it?" she asked in an annoyed tone.

"I didn't say anything," I responded in a near shout.

On that note, we did in fact go home, as Misty was convinced that I had suggested.

Late that night, Misty woke me up in a panic. "Tina was whimpering like before," she spoke softly.

"Then, just before I came to tell you, she kept saying *I can't, I can't, I can't.*"

I sat up in bed, and thought for a moment, without replying. "Come on, quietly," I instructed Misty.

We both snuck back into her room. Tina was still in bed and appeared to me sleeping peacefully now. We stood there watching her sleep for a long time. Nothing happened. I motioned Misty back to my room. "She seems ok now. How about, if it happens again, you come get me, and we will wake her up," I suggested.

Misty wasn't having it. "I can't sleep in there, I'm scared," she whined.

I couldn't blame her, after everything that had happened. I thought for a second. "Ok, you sleep in my bed, and I will sleep in your bed," I offered, "just for tonight."

I went and laid down in Misty's bed. The girls' room felt at least ten degrees hotter than mine. My bedroom had two windows that led into the backyard. The girls' room only had one window that led onto the front porch and was blocked off by shelves. It was pointless to even open their window. I was so uncomfortable that I could not sleep. The good news is that Tina was sleeping, without any issues.

A couple of hours had passed when I heard a loud rattling noise outside of the room. I slowly got up and stepped outside of my sister's bedroom into the hallway. There was another rattle. It was coming from my bedroom. Immediately, I thought it was Misty going through my stuff. I rushed into the room to catch her, and I did.

When I opened the door, I expected to find Misty in my piggy bank, or perhaps the toy box. Instead, my sister was sitting on the edge of my bed, with her feet dangling out of the window. The screen had been removed.

I closed my bedroom door and flipped on the light switch. Misty twisted her body to face me but said nothing. It looked as though she were sleeping with her eyes open. "What are you doing?!" I screamed in a whisper.

Misty didn't respond. She turned back around and looked out of the window. I wondered if she was considering ignoring me. It was a five-foot drop from the window. She would be fine if she jumped, but I'm sure it seemed scary to a little girl. The real question was, where would she go; and why?

I waited for a few seconds, trying to understand what was happening. Finally, I'd had enough. I grabbed Misty by the shoulders and pulled her back in from the window sill. Laying on the bed she looked up at me. I could see the fear in her eyes. She had no reason to be scared of me, just for pulling her in. She sat up on the bed silently, and tucked her knees under her arms as if she were cold. There was a bit of chill in the air outside, so it made sense I thought.

"Why were you jumping out of my window?" I asked Misty as if I were tired of waiting for an answer.

Misty began to cry softly, "I don't want to be here anymore, I'm scared."

My defenses immediately dropped, and I felt my anger dissipate. "There is nothing to be afraid of. You can't be afraid of Tina. She just had a bad dream probably, that's all," I tried to assure her.

Misty sniffled and wiped snot from her nose onto my sheets, "I'm not scared of Tina," she said.

I internally sighed a breath of relief, too soon. Misty continued, "I'm afraid of it."

"What?" I asked, clearly confused.

A second of silence passed between us, "I'm afraid of the calling."

I wanted to tell Misty that the calling wasn't real. However, since my experience, I wasn't so sure. I was a bit foggy after my injury, but I remembered seeing something in the farmhouse with Tina. I remember feeling a coldness just before Tina plunged a butcher knife into my stomach. I thought that there was plenty to be frightened of.

"As long as we stay away from the farmhouse, I think that we will be ok," I apprised Misty.

I tried to hug Misty, but my arms were too short to fit around her with her knees stuck in her chest. I had a distinct feeling that I had not comforted her at all, and that she had something more to tell me. It was written on her face.

"I heard it today," Misty mumbled.

"What?" I asked, praying that there was a misunderstanding.

She looked up to me for the first time. She looked me right in the eyes. It was almost as if she could see through me. "I heard the calling," she said.

My heart sank, and I was sure that my face had gone white. I thought back to the incident in the fort when Misty accused me of saying I wanted to go home. I remembered Tina telling us that she was called to *come home*. Until that moment I had forgotten what she said to me at the farmhouse, *I am home*.

I would not ignore the happening this time. I needed to get ahead of it, and stay ahead of it. I needed to know exactly what Misty had heard. "You heard the calling at the fort?" I asked Misty.

She nodded her head. "What exactly did it say to you?" I continued my interrogation.

"At first, I thought it was you. I thought it said go home," Misty recalled.

"Then, I heard it louder and more clearly, it said *come home*," Misty shuddered.

Ok, I thought, this was good. At least both girls were hearing the same thing. We wouldn't have to fight on two fronts, and maybe our grandparents would believe us; since both of them were hearing it.

I stood looking out the open window, considering what we should do, and how we should do it. A breeze picked up and came into the room. Misty pulled my blanket up over her. I thought about her, just leaving in the middle of the night, wearing nothing but her nightgown, and taking no supplies. It didn't make sense.

"Misty, where were you going once you left the house?" I asked.

She shrugged, "I dunno."

I got the sense that her answer was not entirely true. "Were you running away on your own, or were you being called?" I asked slowly.

Misty started to sniffle again, and I knew the answer before she responded, "it was the calling."

Just then, I heard a movement outside of my door. I turned to the door and then froze, waiting for something to happen. I realized that my nerves were probably getting the best of me, and then expected Tina to open my door, wondering why the light was on, and what we were doing. Another moment passed, and no one entered. I opened my door myself, just in time to hear the lock clicking on the front door.

My grandparents had decided to begin locking the doors at night. They thought this might help keep us kids in the house, in case we hatched another plan to leave during the night. They apparently did not understand that we were all capable of unlocking the door from the inside, and I knew that they did not appreciate the seriousness of what was happening. I hoped that they would when it was time.

I made my way carefully through the living room and looked out of the wide-open front door. There was a security light on the front porch, and I could see Tina leaving the front yard. You must be kidding me, was all I could think. I ran out to the front yard to stop her. I reminded myself to approach with caution, in case she was wielding another knife.

I called out from behind, "Tina stop!"

To my surprise, she complied. She turned around to face me, and then asked, "what are you doing out here?"

In desperation, I responded, "saving you."

Tina responded matter-of-factly, "saving me from what? I'm just going home."

I dropped to my knees and began to cry uncontrollably. What was happening to my sisters? Why was this happening? Tina came to me and kneeled beside me, draping her arm on my shoulder. I did not even care if she had another weapon, I just wanted this to be over. Tina whispered to me, "shhhh, it's ok, let's go back inside."

We headed back to the house, and Misty was waiting on the front porch. We stood there for several minutes all holding hands, in an unplanned circle. Not a word was spoken. The sun would be rising in a few minutes, and it was almost time to start the day. We went into the kitchen, and my sisters got down bowls and spoons for cereal.

I had tried to handle this situation but had failed. Not only had I been stabbed by my youngest sister, but now I was losing both of them. It was time. I woke up Grandma and Granddaddy, and asked them to join us at the table.

We told them everything.

2020

I trudged slowly back to the trailer where my campsite, and car were. Moments after arriving, puking, and chugging a bottle of water,

Uncle Ray pulled up on his tractor. "Oh boy, I can tell just by looking at ya, that you aint gonna be worth nothin this mornin," my uncle mocked me.

I hadn't even asked my uncle for help, nor did I recall telling him that I intended to begin removing the trailer today. I figured I would start taking apart the front porch, which I knew would be difficult alone. The front porch was very well built, but also poorly maintained. As such, part of it was solid, and part of it was falling apart. Ray was always the first to lend a helping hand, and I shouldn't have been surprised. His tractor would make much quicker work of pulling the porch down and moving it to the fire pit.

Uncle Ray had also brought me up a small breakfast snack. I wasn't sure if I could stomach it, but I knew that I needed it. I opened the front passenger door on my rental to grab another bottle of water to wash down breakfast with. In the front seat was the stack of pictures I had removed from the trailer walls yesterday. Sitting right on top was the picture of my grandmother as a child. I pulled it out from the car to show to Ray.

"Look what I found hanging in the house," I showed Ray.

"Oh yeah, I made one for your mama too," he chuckled, "after she died, I asked Tina if she wanted it, but she said no thanks," Ray shrugged it off.

I thought to myself, God had never made a more thoughtful man. Then, I turned the frame over and looked at the chicken scratched letters that spelled out *come home*. I was almost afraid to ask, "did you do this too?" I showed Ray the frame.

He took the picture from me and inspected it closely. "No, I didn't do that. *Come home,* he read the scratched-out letters."

A huge gust of wind nearly blew the frame right out of his hands, "boy, that is creepy," he handed me back the frame, and climbed onto his tractor, "where do you wanna start?"

10

There is more than One Way to Skin a Cat

1992

As I expected, our grandparents thought that most of our tale was nonsense. The only premise that they seemed to accept was that the girls must have been sleepwalking. I had to show them my window as proof that Misty had tried to leave too. The discussion ended with us all being grounded, as if that would fix the problem. Either they didn't understand, didn't care, or they knew something that we did not.

When we got home from school that afternoon, we discovered that both the front and the back doors had deadbolts near the top. Well out of reach from any of us kids, the brass locks signified our imprisonment. The lock could only be worked with a key, and I couldn't help but think that it was a pretty good solution. It should definitely keep the girls in the house at night, but would it also keep *her* out?

That weekend my Granddaddy, and Uncle Mark installed steel bars on all of the windows. While the new locks served as a symbol of our imprisonment, the bars made it a reality. It never occurred to the adults, what might happen if the girls felt trapped. If the spirit were denied. For me, locking us in at night was only a solution for a symptom. The real problem waited at the farmhouse.

The following week was uneventful. I didn't sleep much because I was waiting for something to happen. I could sense that this was not over yet. We were grounded to the front yard, and we could not even see the farmhouse, which I figured was probably a good thing.

It was two weeks to the day from the last happening that I was awakened by a loud banging sound. I got out of bed and made my way down the hall. I stopped by my sister's room and poked my head in. Whatever was happening, my sisters were both up too. I entered the living room at the same time as my grandmother. We both looked at each other shocked by what we saw.

Grandma, pushed back through the kitchen to wake up Granddaddy who was insulated in the back room. In the meantime, I called out to my sisters, "Misty...Tina...wake up!" I hollered as if that were the problem.

They did not acknowledge me at all. They continued banging and kicking on the front door. Now they began screaming too, "Let me out! Let me out!"

Granddaddy and Grandma rejoined me in the living room. I looked at Granddaddy who had his pistol in his hand. I jumped in front of him. "What are you doing?" I bawled.

He laid the pistol on the table, once he had a sense of what was happening. I finally breathed again. I heard Grandma say to Granddaddy, "you aren't supposed to wake up sleepwalkers."

"They aren't sleepwalking!" I nearly screamed at them.

I ran to the girls and grabbed Misty from behind. We both fell to the ground, but when she stood up, she didn't scream, hit, or kick. She was looking dead at me, and our grandparents. Her eyes were dilated so large that they appeared more black than brown. Tina joined her. They just stood there looking at us, and waiting for something. Tina's eyes were not dilated. Instead, her naturally bright blue eyes almost looked like tiny flashlights. They were brighter than I had ever seen them before.

I whispered back towards my grandparents, "they're possessed."

After thirty seconds of trying to kill us with laser beam eyes, they returned to normal. They acted as if nothing had just happened, and asked if they could return to bed. I walked them to their room, laid down, and closed their eyes. It was the saddest thing I had ever seen.

I sat up with my grandparents and talked for some time that night. Seeing is believing, and now they believed that there was something more going on here. They asked me to tell them the entire story again. The more insanity that I shared with them, the quicker they seemed to forget what had just happened. In the end, they accepted that Misty and Tina were both going through some sort of psychosis, but refused to entertain any spirits or haunted houses. Grandma flat out said, "I grew up in that house, and it has been here my entire life, there isn't anything wrong with it."

Tina had a weekly standing appointment with her psychiatrist for ongoing therapy. She had not mentioned anything about the spirit, farmhouse, or the calling since returning home. Grandma had started working only half a day on therapy days so that she could take Tina to her appointments. She complained regularly about missing work and making extra trips into Gainesville.

The next day Grandma scheduled Misty an appointment with the therapist too. Grandma thought that she may be suffering trauma similar to Tina's. She wasn't wrong.

Two more nights that week, the exact events happened. The girls banging and yelling at the front door to get out. One night, Misty tried to break a window. Whether my grandparents realized it or not, the situation was evolving into something more serious. I could sense things turning violent.

During the days, my sisters were as pleasant as ever. Everything seemed completely normal. I think that is what made the situation so difficult to understand. It was getting cooler, the windows had been closed, and the creek was too cold to even stand in. The week that we closed the windows for the season, something changed.

Misty and Tina still had their attempted breakouts regularly. Now, they seemed to have given up on the door. Their focus became the windows. At first, I assumed that they were trying to figure out how to get out of the windows. They should have known that exiting the windows was impossible with the steel bars in place, I thought.

It was a Friday night, and we had stayed up late watching a movie on ABC. By the time the movie was over, we were all exhausted, and ready for bed. I fell asleep as soon as my head hit the pillow. I was in a deep sleep when I was awoken by a loud crash. I woke up dashing towards the sound. I nearly ran over Misty and Tina as I rounded the corner into the living room. They were calmly and quietly walking back to bed. I watched them enter their bedroom, climb back into bed, and close their eyes.

I returned to the living room where my grandmother sat sobbing. It had become too much for her. The girls had broken every window in the living room. They broke the windows, and then went back to bed on their own. It was almost as if they knew they couldn't get out, but they were trying to let something in.

The broken windows were the final straw. The girl's doctors had recommended medicating them at night, but Grandma had declined the treatment. She said it was because she didn't want the girls on drugs, but I think it was really the cost which had made her decision. Now, medication, with their HMO, was cheaper than replacing windows.

The girls and I made a special trip into town on Saturday to go to the Pharmacy. On the way home, I sat in the front passenger seat next to Grandma who was driving. I pulled a bottle of the medication out of the bag, and read the label. One pill by mouth before bedtime, with a glass of water, would make the girls unconscious for up to eight hours. I looked over to Grandma while still holding the bottle. I noticed a tear stream down her cheek. This was as messed up as I thought it was. I dropped the bottle back into the bag and spent the rest of the ride home in silent reflection.

When we got home, we discovered Granddaddy had been busy. The girls now had a new bedroom door. It was solid oak, with a lock to match the front door. He had also installed bars on the inside of their window. Their room was officially a prison cell. It was wrong. Then again, what was right? Everything seemed wrong now.

Between the medication, and the prison cell, the approach seemed to work. A month passed incident-free. Everyone in the house felt a renewed sense of refreshment, and ease. Occasionally, we would forget the medication, and the girls would end up banging around in their room trying to get out, but nothing was broken, and no one got hurt.

The week before Christmas, our Uncle Ray and Aunt Tojuanna came up for a visit. There were some hellos and tickles, and then the children went back to playing while the adults had their small talk. The adults were sitting inside, while us kids played with building blocks, and die-cast cars on the porch. After a few minutes, Aunt Tojuanna came outside to sit with us. When she was finished investigating what we were playing on the porch, Aunt Tojuanna invited us to the truck for a surprise.

What a surprise it was. She had a kitten in her truck. Misty and Tina fell in love immediately. I had to admit, she was super cute. She was solid white, like Sam I thought, but was very playful. I had never seen a kitten before and did not understand that all kittens are playful. Misty and Tina played with the kitten in the bed of the truck for a few minutes before I asked if I could hold her. It seemed as though the kitten did not want to leave the girls, and she was as obsessed with them, as they were with her. Misty scooped up the cat and tried to hand her to me. The kitten did not want to let go or come to me.

Once I finally got a hold of the kitten, I understood why the girls became enthralled so quickly. She was very soft and cuddly. I petted her a few times, and then rubbed her against my face. I was admiring her fur, and checking her out more closely when I noticed her bright blue eyes flash red. Suddenly, she reached out and scratched my face, hard.

During the commotion, she sprung from my hands and ran right back to my sisters for protection. I was trying to stifle back tears, while Tojuanna got some tissue from the truck to tend to my scratches. I looked at the cat angrily, she just sat in my sister's lap purring as she glared at me.

Misty asked Tojuanna, "Where did you get her from?"

"We just found her wandering around up by the Green House," Tojuanna replied.

My sisters asked, "do you mean that she's a stray cat?"

I had other questions that would have to wait. The Green House was a hundred feet from the farmhouse, and no one lived in either. This was a kitten, so where was its mother? How could there be a stray kitten in the middle of a three-hundred-acre farm, with no cats, in the middle of winter?

My thoughts were interrupted by more questions from my sisters, "are you going to keep it?"

Aunt Tojuanna replied, "well, I duuunnnnooooo," in a playful tone.

That tone told me the true intent of this visit. They were trying to give us a cat. More specifically they were trying to give the girls a kitten. I imagined Uncle Ray was inside right now appealing to his sister about how much the girls have been through, and how they need a cat right now.

As if they read my mind, Uncle Ray emerged from the porch followed by Grandma and Granddaddy. They all had come to see the girls playing with the new kitten. Misty did not hesitate, for even a second, telling Grandma everything she knew about the kitten.

Then Aunt Tojuanna chimed in, "well, I would give her to you girls, if it's ok with your Grandma."

Just like that, the gates had been opened. The begging, appeal, and promise's that poured from the back of the truck was almost sickening. Perhaps I was being harsh. Everyone else seemed to love the kitten. Maybe I would give her another chance. The fact that my grandparents came outside to see the kitten, told me that the decision had already been made. We now owned a cat.

The one rule that Grandma had for the girls, was that the kitten was to be an outdoor cat. The furthest she was allowed to come into the house, was the front porch. A week later, we got a cold snap that changed that. The girls begged and pleaded that it was too cold to leave a baby kitten outside. From then on, the cat was allowed in the girls' room only.

Misty and Tina had a tough time agreeing on a name for the cat. I couldn't care less because it was clear by this point that the cat hated me, and I hated it. Something about her eyes. They were bright blue against her white fur, which seemed oddly familiar, but when she looked at me, I could swear that her eyes would go red. The girls refuted my claim because she was the softest, cutest, cuddliest kitten that ever lived. After much debate, they finally decided on a name for their new pet. They named her after our Old Grandma who had died a few years before. The cat's name would be Ernestine. I was reminded of the night the girls broke the windows, they weren't trying to get out, *she* wanted to be let in.

2020

By the end of the first day, we had most of the front porch torn down. I was feeling much better after sweating, most of the poison I had drunk the night before, from my body. It had been an eventful day. I had been through three chainsaw chains, stepped on two nails, and Uncle Ray had nearly flipped the tractor over a couple of times.

The sixty-seven-year-old man was working me under the table. No breaks. He just kept going. I tried to pretend that it was the hangover that was slowing me down, but I could tell now how soft the Army had made me.

The last part of the porch to remove was the floor. I had knocked out most of the support beams with the sledgehammer. Fine, Ray had knocked out most of the support beams with the sledgehammer, and now we were just going to try to pull the entire rest of the porch onto the fire with the tractor. Ray took several cracks at it, revving the engine on his ancient small Ford tractor. It was budging, and inch at a time. Something would have to give soon, either the tractor, or the porch.

The porch finally gave way. The success renewed my energy, and I ran around cheering momentarily as Ray slowly pulled the fully intact one-hundred-foot porch floor across the field to the fire. Once he had pulled the floor directly over the fire, I released all of the chains, then we backed away and watched it burn.

Honestly, I was shocked. I could not believe that we had gone all day without seeing one snake. As a child, and maybe an adult too, I always had a strange feeling that there was something scary under the porch. I assumed there would be a snake bed. I had never been so happy to be wrong.

As it got too hot to stand anywhere near the fire while it raged, we walked back over to the trailer. Where the porch once stood was only a strip of sand now. For the first time, I noticed, and recalled the bars on the trailer windows. The trailer had always been so dark, and I realized now it was because the front porch blocked most of the light from getting in. Everything looked different now.

The sand that was under the porch was very dry, and loose. There were a couple of toys that had somehow ended up under the porch, but not nearly as many as I might have guessed. I walked along shifting the sand around with my foot looking for treasure until I found something. It wasn't treasure. Spread around under the porch, covered in the sand, were hundreds of small bones. It did not take me long to figure out what they were.

11

The Spirit isn't Dead, She can Spread

1993

Misty and Tina got so that they could barely stand to leave Ernestine, even to go to school. They would let her outside in the morning just before we left for school, and she would be waiting on the steps for them when we got home. My sisters would immediately scoop her up, take her in their room, and close the door. I barely saw them anymore, and we never played together.

Perhaps I was just jealous. More than likely I was lonely. I tried, on occasion, to go into the girl's room to play with them. The smell in their room was nearly unbearable. When I could come in to play, the cat would dash under the bed. Pretty soon the girls would become too preoccupied with trying to get the cat to come out, to focus on any real play. I would leave.

I would also try to get them to leave their room to play. Rarely would they agree, and never for more than a few minutes. They argued that poor Ernestine had been left alone all day, and is lonely. I thought the shiny object syndrome might wear off soon, but this continued for months.

One morning in March, we left for school. As usual, Ernestine was sitting on the porch stairs, watching us drive away. We were halfway to school when Tina realized that she had forgotten her backpack. Surprisingly, Grandma turned around to go back home, and get it. As we made the turn at the big oak, something caught my eye. It was Ernestine. She was walking toward the green blockhouse and the farmhouse. I didn't say anything to the girls. I hoped that Ernestine had had enough, and was moving on, or back home, wherever that was. Tina did notice that her cat was not sitting on the stairs at the house when she ran inside to get her backpack. "You thought she literally just sat there all day waiting for you?" I offered sarcastically.

When we got home that evening, Ernestine was waiting, as always, on the stairs for her girls. I was sad to say that I was disappointed. I began wondering if she wandered up there every day. If she did, why? What did she do up there all day? If she liked it up there, then why come back here?

Since the girls refused to play with me as usual, and it was warm again now, I decided to take a walk around to see what had changed over the winter. The answer was easy; nothing. Nothing ever changed here. The forts were still intact, although sadly unused. The creek had only the smallest of a trickle of water running through it, as it was dry season. The train tracks had not changed course. I picked up a couple of rocks, put them into my pocket, and pretended I didn't know what for.

Then, the real intent of this walk, the farmhouse. Still standing, and still filled with crap, it watched me mockingly. It actually looked like more junk had been added. Against my better judgment, I jumped up on to the porch. I looked in through the doorway, expecting something or someone. I looked down at my feet. The old wood was stained with a spackle of what I could safely assume were my blood drops.

I felt angry. I began berating the house as though it could hear me. "Why are you doing this? What did we ever do to you?" I asked questions that no one could ever answer.

I began silently crying to myself. I wanted her to show up right now and explain herself. I didn't care if I got hurt again, but I needed to understand at least. Finally, once I realized that no one was coming, I climbed down from the porch and backed up under the pecan tree. I pulled out the rocks I had saved from the railroad. Two large granite rocks. Two curses. I hurled each of them at the house as hard as I could. I hope that you rot. You should be burned to the ground.

Nothing happened of course, but I somehow felt a little better. I hung my head and headed home no smarter than I had left. As I entered the front yard Misty ran out to greet me, I lit up with excitement hoping she wanted to play. "Tommy, come quick, we need you."

It wasn't play, but need was the next best thing. I followed Misty into the house but lost hope as she headed for her bedroom. We entered the room, and she closed the door. The stench was nauseating. Since it had warmed up, they had opened the window in the room, but it did very little to help. "I think Ernestine just had a seizure," Misty reported.

I looked over to Tina who was sitting on her bed stroking the cat. Misty continued, "she was laying on my chest, and then she just starting convulsing, as if someone were beating her."

I looked more closely at the cat. "Now, look at her eyes, they're all bloodshot and red," Tina cried.

I bent down to examine the cat closer. Ernestine hissed and swatted at me, then dashed under the bed. I stood back up and turned to Misty who was already dropping to the floor to get her cat. "Well, she seems better now. I would just keep an eye on her," I said as I exited the room, I doubt anyone heard me or cared.

I had a gut feeling before, but now I was certain. That cat was somehow connected to the farmhouse. I needed to find out how, and why. I needed a plan. I went to my room and closed the door. I spent the night planning ways to defeat the demon, witch, spirit, or whatever it was. I just wanted my sisters back.

The next morning, I pretended to be sick, so I could play hooky from school. It wasn't terribly difficult because I loved going to school, and never tried to play hooky before. Grandma took my temperature and declared that it wasn't that bad. I assured her that I should not go to school. She offered to take the day off, and stay home with me, but I told her that wasn't necessary. I would just lay on the couch, rest, and watch the boob tube.

I made sure that both girls had their backpacks, and then I watched from the window as the van turned at the big oak. Once they were out of sight, I stayed at the window until I spotted Ernestine sauntering across the field. I wanted to give her space so that she didn't see me, and scare off. I was fairly certain that I knew where she was heading.

I ran to the shed to retrieve the tool I would need, and then headed towards the farmhouse. I approached from behind the bales of hay which I had used for cover months before. I peeked around the corner just in time to see Ernestine hop up onto the porch, and enter the house. Creepy cat I thought. Then I reminded myself, it isn't a cat.

I waited. I had all day to get this job done, there was no need to rush, and make a mistake. I waited and watched for over an hour. Nothing happened, that I could see, inside of the house. Ernestine had not left either, not on this side at least.

I emerged from my cover and approached the house. The was no point in trying to be sneaky. I was certain that she knew I was here. "Ernestine, show yourself. Come out here," I beckoned.

I waited for a good long minute before I announced, "fine then, I'm coming in."

Tool in hand, I hopped up on the front porch and stood in the same doorway that I had last summer. "I just want to talk," I shouted to the house.

I waited for a second, and then added, "I want some answers."

I stood in the doorway waiting. She didn't show, but I didn't budge either. I continue scanning the room for the cat, or anything else that might seem abnormal. Two or three minutes of eeriness passed until I was done begging. I announced, "fine we will do this the hard way then."

I raised the saw that I had brought from the shed to the doorframe, and placed the serrated blade against the wood, "last chance!"

I hesitated for a moment. Maybe this was a dumb idea. Perhaps it was just a coincidence that the cat had a reaction at the same time I was throwing rocks at the house. Maybe all of this was just something that I had fabricated in my mind to reconcile my injuries, and sisters not wanting to play with me anymore. One thing was for certain, I wanted this house gone.

I pulled the saw across the grain, and it barely broke the skin of the old wood. I stopped for a second to see if anything would happen. When it didn't, I began sawing fanatically. I was only about a quarter of an inch into the frame when there came a loud, and terrible screeching.

I hopped back from the doorway onto the porch. The last thing I wanted was to get stabbed again, or worse. The screeching lasted for five seconds or so. It was not a human screech, nor a cat screech. It was indescribable for an eleven-year-old.

I stepped back into the doorway searching for evidence of the screech. "Show yourself!" I hollered again.

There was no response. I realized that there was only one way that she would listen to me. I put the saw back into the groove I had begun cutting in the doorway. I looked around one last time and then began working the saw again. When the screeching started, I didn't stop. I kept right on sawing. I was over half an inch through the frame now. I continued sawing as the screech got louder and longer. As I broke through the frame, and into the wall, a bright light appeared at the far end of the kitchen.

I stopped sawing but left the blade in the wood. I was scared stiff and didn't know what to do. When I stopped sawing, the screeching stopped, but the light remained. I began cutting again, and the light grew larger. All of the anger and fear that I had been carrying inside of me since last summer boiled over as I sawed furiously. The light began to move toward me, and grow larger. It picked up speed as it came, and quickly transformed into the lady I had seen before. She was charging me. I couldn't help but think she looked just like Sam the bull when he was charging me. They had an identical look in their eye. I stumbled back onto the porch and fell to the ground as I watched her rush through the doorway.

As she exited the house, which I had not expected, she turned into Ernestine. The cat pounced on me clawing away. I managed the get a hold of her at the right time, and throw her at the pecan tree. I knew what I needed to do.

I jumped back onto the porch, grabbed the saw, and went at it. As I sawed into the wall, Ernestine began flopping around and spasming on the ground. She was dying. I sawed and sawed. It felt like my arm might fall off. I sawed until Ernestine stopped moving. The cat laid sprawled out on the ground under the pecan tree motionless. I collapsed on the porch.

I sat there for a minute catching my breath. My eyes did not leave Ernestine. It occurred to me that I had my back to the door, which caused me to jump up. I climbed down from the porch, and approached the cat carefully. I watched it closely. It was not breathing. It was not moving. It was dead.

I used a gray loose board to scoop the cat up and put her under the house. No one really ever came up this way, and I doubted that anyone would spot it. Just in case, I laid the board on top of the cat, to conceal it. I got the saw, then looked back at the house one more time.

I began to walk away, and looked back again, wondering if I had really killed it. I was sure that the cat was dead, but was the spirit, or the house. When I looked back someone else caught my eye. Standing between the barn, and the farmhouse was my Uncle Philip. He was staring at the house when I noticed him. Then he transitioned his distant stare directly at me. I waved and wondered how long he had been there. Neither of us spoke.

That evening when the girls got home from school, and Ernestine wasn't waiting for them, they were frantic. For the first time since getting that cat, they were outside doing something, which was hopeful for me. I helped them search. They were certain that Ernestine would come to them when called.

After we had searched the entire immediate area around the house with no luck, the girls decided to expand their search. To be concise, they were no longer actually searching. They seemed to know right where she would be, and they marched off toward the farmhouse. I begged the girls to slow down and consider if this was a good idea. They did not appear to be worried in the least, and there was no stopping them.

I was partially worried that they would find Ernestine dead and obviously covered by a board. I was more apprehensive that we might never get them out of the house if they went inside. They were practically running as I tried to reason with them. When they reached sight of the farmhouse they began calling again, "Ernestine, come here girl."

When Misty and Tina reached the front yard, I expected them to stop, and survey the house from a distance first. They did not. The girls immediately jumped up onto the porch and entered the house. As Tina walked into the kitchen, she stopped and grabbed the doorframe. It was over I thought. They would take Tina away again. Tina just said, "she's hurt."

When Tina removed her hand from the frame, and entered the dwelling, I noticed that she had been holding the frame right where I had made my cut. The girls called and called, and pushed things out of the way in hopes of exposing the cat. While they were occupied, I glanced around the corner to where I had hidden Ernestine. The board was lying there, but the cat was gone. My mind raced. There was no way, I thought, that the cat was alive. I saw it. I moved it. It was dead. Then it occurred to me that maybe Uncle Philip had seen the cat, and buried it. I should have buried it myself I thought.

Suddenly, the cat calling coming from inside of the house stopped. I rushed back around the house and looked through the doorway. Both of my sisters were still standing in the kitchen, neither making a sound, and both looking up. I called to them, "Misty...Tina, come on, she isn't here, let's go."

The girls didn't move an inch or acknowledge me. They stayed where they stood, and continued looking up. I remembered the words Misty showed me scratched into the kitchen ceiling. I had not noticed the words since that day, but I had not really looked either. I wanted to look now, but I was terrified.

Finally, they lowered their heads, turned around, and exited the house. I was thankful. "We will find her," I said, "she just isn't here."

As the girls passed me, Tina stopped and glared at me for only five seconds, but I could sense the hatred in her heart. She then rejoined her sister, in walking home. Neither said a word to me the entire walk. When we got to the trailer, they went directly to their room and shut the door.

That night was horrible. All night the girls banged, and beat on anything they could find. They screamed bloody murder to let them out, and let them go home. My grandparents assumed the girls had forgotten to take their medicine. Knowing the situation, I had made sure that they took it. Accidentally giving them another dose could have serious consequences, I reminded them. As long as they were making noise, we assumed that they were physically fine. It was a long night.

The next day, on the way to school, the girls no longer looked so angry. They appeared exhausted. I thought, even if they didn't take their medication tonight, they were going to sleep like babies. Me too. It was a long day.

That evening I was somewhat surprised that the girls didn't want to look for Ernestine. I was bored but afraid to go to sleep too early and mess up the slumber that I had planned. I knocked on the girl's door, which was unlocked. It had been very quiet since we had gotten home. The door gently opened, and Misty answered with no words. "Do you guys wanna go look for Ernestine?" I asked trying not to sound guilty.

Misty simply responded, "no thank you," and closed the door.

I wasn't sure what was going on. That was nothing new I thought. Either the girls had given up, were very angry at me, or they knew something that I didn't know. I suspected that it was a combination of the latter two. Honestly, I hoped that it wasn't that the girls had given up. If all of us gave up, then we would surely be doomed.

That night before an early bedtime, my grandparents watched me give the girls their medication. It occurred to me that perhaps they weren't really swallowing the pills, and were throwing them away in their room. After they finished chasing the pills with water, I asked them to open their mouths. They did so without hesitation, and I found nothing.

I fell asleep immediately, and so did my sisters. Until midnight that is. Then they unleashed hell. It somehow sounded worse than the night before. How was this possible, I wondered? It was so bad that I wished Ernestine was still here. I took my pillow and blanket and made a pallet on the floor in the backroom. It wasn't hot enough to run the air conditioner yet, so I could still hear the girls, if I listened close. Eventually, I fell asleep, and forgot the terrible nightmare that we were living.

By breakfast, the girls were covered in bruises. It was therapy day, and Grandma would have to report what was happening. I wasn't sure it would help but was willing to hope. I did not go to the sessions, and I typically did not know what happened there. I half expected the doctors to keep the girls for observation. Actually, I hoped that they would. I could not have imagined what would happen.

When the girls got home, they went straight to their room, as usual. Unexpectedly, I was summoned to the kitchen table by my grandparents, which I knew could not be a good thing. The doctor said that the girl's outburst was my fault. The girls told her that I had killed Ernestine. They weren't wrong, but how could they know. I flat out denied the claim to my grandparents, and they seemed to believe me. They didn't appear angry, they actually seemed sad. Then the other shoe dropped. I had an appointment with the therapist next week.

The doctor increased the dosage of the girl's medication, and it seemed to work. It was a relatively quiet night. The next day was Friday, and I was looking forward to ending the week on a good note. The bus dropped us off at the railroad tracks, and we walked home. The girls seemed to be in a good mood and were giggling. I decided to test my luck, "you guys wanna check out the fort for a minute?" I asked.

To my surprise, they agreed. For fifteen minutes it felt as it were before. We shared ideas of ways to make the fort better, laughed, and played. It wasn't much, but it was a start. I tried to keep up the small talk for the rest of the way home. The girls appeased me, but it felt forced to me. When we reached the front yard, I was stopped in my tracks. The girls ran to the porch with an expected excitement. Ernestine was sitting on the stairs as if she had been there the entire time, waiting for the girls. Beside her, sat a new friend. A solid black cat; with red eyes.

2020

As I pushed around the sand with a shovel, I uncovered more and more cat skeletons. I recalled as a child, getting a kitten for Christmas. Somehow, one cat had turned into dozens. One day, when I was fifteen years old, I took a picture in the back yard of thirty-seven cats, lounging in the sun. I always wondered what had happened to them, and where they had gone. I looked up at the trailer and made a realization. All of the cat bones were scattered around the window to my sisters' childhood bedroom.

Uncle Ray was sitting under the carport in the shade drinking sweet tea from a jug that he had brought from his house. I joined him, and he pushed over a chair for me to have a seat. It was inviting, but I had too much on my mind now. "Hey, Uncle Ray, do you remember all of those cats that used to run around here when I was a kid?" I asked.

"Oh sure, we used to call this the cat farm," he laughed.

He looked around as if he had just noticed, "I guess they all live in the woods now that you ain't here to feed em no more," he realized.

"Well, not all of em anyway. Come check this out," I said as I snatched back up the shovel, and motioned to where the porch had been.

Ray followed me without complaint or question. When we approached the window, I turned back to Ray, and joked, "don't scream."

I stirred the dirt up a little right in front of the window. Then I moved back a few steps, swept the dirt away there too. I made eye contact with Uncle Ray, and there was visible confusion on both of our faces. There was nothing there.

12

Guilty

I swung open the door, and the near artic temperature blasted my skin. My vision took a second to correct itself from the blinding natural sunlight to the dimly lit office. I could not believe how cold this building was. I had been conditioned to automatically wonder what their electric bill must be. My sisters rushed past me claiming toys that were set up in the corner of the waiting room. They had been here a dozen times.

I sort of lingered in the doorway trying to make sense of my surroundings. My sisters had run off to the right, and my grandmother split off to the left. She was already at the front desk speaking with a large woman, who handed Grandma some paperwork. Other than that, there were only two other people in the waiting room. A mother and daughter, I presumed, sat quietly and motionless. The little girl kept her head low, but I could tell that she was watching my sisters play. I wanted to invite her to join them, but I had a feeling my offer would not be accepted.

Instead, I just found an empty chair and sat down alone. I did not understand why now, after more than six months of the girl's therapy, the doctors wanted to see me. I had not suffered from any of the trauma that my sisters had experienced. I felt like the focus should be on making my sisters well again. Maybe the doctors think that I can help, I hoped.

My grandmother must have finished the paperwork because she came and sat next to me empty-handed. She didn't say a word as she sat beside me and pulled a romance novel from her purse. I always wondered how a deeply devoted Christian woman like her could read so many books with half-dressed people of the cover. I was slightly embarrassed and checked to see if the other woman sitting across from us had noticed.

I began wondering if my Grandma and Granddaddy had to do these sessions too. If I had to, it would make sense that they should too. I was just about to ask her when the door swung open, and a young girl walked out from the back. It was not difficult to tell that she was related to the only other people sitting in the room. I watched her mother and sister stand up to join the girl, and the family exited the office together. I was speculating on why the family might be here when I heard a soft voice call my name, "Tommy, we are ready for you whenever you are ready."

I was suddenly certain that I wasn't ready. I wanted to leave. I could feel my hands trembling. I felt like I had something to hide. Something that this head doctor would learn soon enough. Then what? Maybe they would take me away. Maybe I would spend the rest of my life in a padded cell, being fed through a straw. I was only a kid!

Grandma gave me a nudge, and I stood up sheepishly. I expected my knees to give out, and collapse back into the chair, but they held up. I headed towards the door. I gave one last glance towards my sisters, who were playing quietly in the corner, and paying no mind to me. I don't know why, but I felt compelled to say something, "goodbye," I offered to no response.

I assumed that the lady leading me back to the examination room was a nurse. She was wearing scrubs, but maybe she was just the front desk lady. She was a heavy-set black woman who exuded joy in her work. She talked the entire walk back to the doctor's office, and kept putting her hand on my shoulders, and ruffling my hair.

She gave a quick rap on a mostly closed door. I took the moment to read the plate which was fastened to the wall next to the door: Dr. Laura Winders. Something about the name relaxed me. Maybe it was because the doctor was a woman I wondered.

The nurse/receptionist pushed the door all of the way open so that I could see the room on the other side. The room did not look like the rest of the building, which appeared to just be cinder blocks painted white. I expected an examination table, rubber gloves, tools to poke and prod with. I didn't see any of that.

The room had large windows for viewing a small pond outside that I had not noticed before. One wall was completely hidden by enormous bookshelves with large fancy-looking books that no one could ever possibly read. I scanned down to the shelf second from the bottom and noticed the lower shelf was filled with children's books. They somehow seemed more reasonable. The other end of the room looked like a playpen. There was a Lego table, stuffed animals, toy cars, and dolls. In the center of the room was a big comfortable chair facing two smaller, yet equally comfortable looking chairs.

Somehow, I didn't notice the lady until last. She was leaning against her desk as if she were waiting for me to be impressed. Once my eyes fell upon her, she stood up and walked toward me. She may have been the tallest woman that I have ever seen. She had dark curly hair to match her dark complexion. It struck me odd that she was wearing a doctor's coat, with her name stitched on it and all, but had no stethoscope or any other tools of the trade, that I could see. What I remember most about Dr. Winders, were her full painted lips. I had just begun noticing women, and it would be a long time before I forgot these lips.

"Good afternoon Tommy," she introduced herself, "my name is Laura, come on in."

The nurse pulled the door shut behind me as I crossed into the room. I suddenly felt trapped when the door clicked shut. I could not help but look back. This was it I thought, my last chance to run.

A hand fell lightly on my shoulder, "would you like to sit down?" the doctor offered.

With that small touch and simple gesture, my anxiety melted away for the moment. I wanted to be in the room. I looked up to the doctor who was smiling brightly to me and nodded my head. I did want to talk to her.

I was tempted to take the big chair, just to see what she might do, but so far things were friendly, and I decided not to jeopardize that. As I took my seat, the doctor turned to her desk to pick up a notebook and a pen, and then she sat across from me.

The setting seemed inviting to me. I was glad that she didn't sit behind her desk. It would feel like I was in trouble at the principal's office. "Do you like to be called Tommy?" she asked.

A simple harmless question, with so many implications. I had never been asked that before. Occasionally, people would call me Tom, but for the most part, everyone called me Tommy. I knew that I was putting way too much thought into this, and taking too long to respond. But my response would set the tone for how she thought of me and spoke to me for the rest of our time together. It was important that I got it right. Stick with Tommy, which was what was comfortable to me, or go with Tom, and signify my manhood.

"Actually, I go by Tom," I finally responded.

As soon as I said it, it felt wrong. She scratched out something on her notepad and wrote a note. "It's nice to finally meet you Tom, please call me Laura," she offered, looking me right in the eye.

She saw right through Tom. I slunk down in my chair a little. I was still Tommy.

She started small, "how was school today?"

I could not remember the last time I was asked that question. "It was fine," I offered.

She laughed away my shortness, "what is your favorite class?"

I sat back up in my chair as big as I could make myself, "American history," I responded more confidently.

"That is mine too!" she offered warmly as I scanned the books behind to tell if she were lying.

Most of the books just had numbers on the spines, but I doubted that they were history books. I decided not to challenge her. She switched into another gear, "you have had quite a year, how are you doing?"

How am I doing? Well, let's see, I got stabbed by my little sister who has apparently lost her mind, I can barely sleep, I live with demon cats who hate me, and no one believes me that it is all caused by a haunted house. "I'm good," the lie caused me to shift in my seat.

The doctor wrote something down. "Are you all healed from your stomach injury?" she asked.

"Yes ma'am, I don't feel a thing," I answered honestly.

"That's so great," she made another quick note, "and how about your sleep?" she was rolling now.

"Uh, I mean, it's ok. Sometimes my sister's sleepwalking keeps me awake," I said using her lingo.

"I am sorry to hear that," she offered, "how does it keep you awake?"

I thought for a second, "just them moving around in their room and banging around, I guess."

"I see. Does that worry you?" she followed up.

"What do you mean? Like afraid that they will get out again?" I asked for clarification.

"Well," she started, then stopped.

"Why are you afraid they will get out?" she rephrased her question.

She chose her words carefully, so I knew that I should too. "I wouldn't want them to disappear again, or hurt themselves."

"They are lucky to have a big brother to worry for them. Do you worry that they might hurt you?" she was now setting up her questions.

I assumed that she wanted me to admit that I was, but I wasn't sure why. "I don't think that they want to hurt anyone," I crafted the perfect response.

"What do you think that they want?" she asked.

I knew that I had to be careful here. If I started ranting about haunted houses, then I would be spending a lot more time with Laura. "They want to leave."

Now Laura paused for a long time writing down a series of notes. I wish I knew what she was writing. I wondered if she was doing it intentionally to make me uncomfortable. "Why do they want to leave?" she finally continued.

I had no idea how to answer this question. They weren't scared. They weren't angry. There was only one honest answer, "they feel called."

"Called by who?" she turned her head sideways as if this were new information to her.

Don't say the house. Don't say the house. I fidgeted in my seat. "They won't say," was all I offered, knowing that my words were hollow.

"Do you ever feel called?" she asked next.

My eyes shot up from the floor to meet hers, "never."

"Why do you think that your sisters hear this calling, but you do not?" she asked flatly.

I just shrugged. I really didn't know. I was just happy that I had not heard the calling yet. I had been in both the water and the house. I had seen things with my own eyes that most people would never believe. But for some reason, I still do not hear the calling.

As if the doctor could read my mind, she asked, "you were with your sisters at each of the happenings: the pond, the swamp, and then of course the house, weren't you?" she asked with what sounded like an accusatory tone to me.

"Yes ma'am," I gulped as quietly as possible.

"Did your sisters seem ok before these incidents?" she asked.

"Yeah, they were fine," I responded, trying to relax myself.

"Which incident did you start to notice a change?" she inquired.

"Tina was different after the pond. I'm not sure when Misty started hearing things. She didn't tell me until the end of summer," I tried to recall accurately.

Again, Laura made a long inscription on her filling page. I sat silently replaying my responses in my head. I thought it was going well. I began to sense a feeling of survival. My thoughts were interrupted, "these noises that you hear at night, coming from your sister's bedroom," she referred to her notes, "you say they are caused by sleepwalking?" she was getting to her point.

"I don't think they are sleepwalking," I said before I could stop myself.

"What are they doing then?" she asked.

"Trying to get out, but I don't think that they are asleep," I offered.

"They are awake?" Laura leaned towards me.

I let out a sigh of frustration, "no."

I had learned not to use the word *possessed*, "they are in a trance."

Laura, who had seemed to be in a trance of her own, readjusted in her seat, apparently dismissing my claim. "Have you ever seen them in this, trance?" she asked.

"Yes," I answered.

"Can you describe it please?" she pressed on.

"Well, it's like they can't hear me. They are completely focused on escaping. And their eyes! Their eyes change too," I stated excitedly.

I had Laura's attention again. I liked it. "How do they break the trance?" she asked with sincerity.

I thought for a moment. Trying to recall precisely what had happened. "I guess when they are satisfied," was the best I could come up with.

"How so?" she nudged me, knowing I knew what she was referring too.

To put it into words was hard, "satisfied that they cannot escape. Satisfied that they have done what they were asked. Satisfied that they have our attention."

Laura sat staring at me for a second. Perhaps she expected me to say something else. I think that she was just as confused as I was. "Oh, um, you used the word *escaped* a couple of times. What do you mean by escaped?"

Now I was the one staring at her. Trying to figure out how much she knew. Surely, she knew about the locks, right? "Trying to escape their room or the house, I guess," was my only response.

"Yes, but why? Why or what are they trying to escape?" she tried to clarify.

"I don't know. I don't think that they are trying to escape from anything. I think that they are trying to escape to something or someone," I tried to explain.

Laura was suddenly reminded of something, "oh yes," she rifled through her notebook, "to this Ernestine person perhaps? Is that your mother?" she asked.

A bit confused myself, "No. My mother's name is Sharon. Ernestine is my great-grandmothers' name," I corrected the doctor.

I could see the information coming back to her, "That's right. Does she live on the farm?"

"Old Grandma has been dead for years," I looked at her blankly.

There was a look of both shock and confusion on the doctor's face. I could tell by her expression that my sisters must speak of Ernestine regularly, as if she were alive. "Oh, you might be thinking of the cat. They named their cat Ernestine."

Laura didn't look certain, but my clarification eased some of the burden from her face. She looked at her watch. "Oh my, you must be good company. The time has flown by. I want to get your sisters in here and talk with them for a few minutes, so we will wrap this up. I have just one more question for you."

I almost made it. I almost survived whatever it is this was supposed to be. However, now I had a feeling that the other shoe was about to drop.

"Tommy, you are the oldest, and you seem very mature for your age," she began by fluffing my ego.

"I am just going to ask you outright because I know that you can be honest with me, and you seem fearless," she was really building up to something.

Laura turned in her chair so that she could set the notepad and pen on her desk. When she turned back to me her smile was gone. If that would have been the first time that she ever looked at me, I would have sworn that she had never smiled before. I noticed that her lips suddenly appeared much smaller.

Laura leaned forward towards me and placed a hand on my knee. I couldn't hear anything that she said, but I read every word from her lips. "Is there any abuse happening in your home?"

I replayed the entire conversation that we had just had. To an eleven-year-old child, that seemed like a hard-left turn. Or was it. She had asked questions about the noises, and trying to escape, but had not mentioned the bruises that covered my sister's arms and legs. She had not mentioned my grandparents even once. She had mentioned my role quite a bit. Did she think that I was abusing Misty and Tina?

Even as a child I understood that times were changing. The mere fact that I was sitting in this office was a clear indication of that. Just a few years before, in the late eighties, my principal kept a thick belt hanging on her wall above her desk. She meant business. I know because I had been on the receiving end of that business many times before.

But it was 1993 now. The wall had fallen. America was changing quickly. Spanking had become taboo overnight. Citizens would rather send a kid to jail, and ruin his life, than spank him accordingly. The government had found authority in the privacy of our own homes. I knew what admitting that we were spanked would do, regardless of whether or not we deserved it.

"No. I saw my sister's cause those bruises themselves. Adults may be too smart to believe it, but something bigger is happening here. Misty and Tina are not crazy, they're being called by something or someone. Instead of pointing fingers, why don't you figure out what or who is causing this?" I was fired up.

"Tommy, that is all I am trying to do," Laura tried to calm me.

I wasn't quite done, "if you want to see what is going on, then why don't you come spend the night?" I asked, trying not to sound pervy.

"Actually, I think that we are having the same thought," Laura stood up.

I followed suit out of habit. She led the way to the door, "it was very nice to meet you Tom," I realized that was the first time she had used the shortened version of my name since the beginning of our conversation, "I hope that we can talk again soon."

The nurse joined us to escort me to the waiting room. During the short walk I thought to myself, I hope that we get to talk again too. I looked back to Laura's office one last time. She was still standing there and gave me a goodbye wave. A hug would have been nice I thought as the door to the waiting room opened for me.

2020

For $12.99 you can buy the best shower in the world from Love's Travel Stop, on the north end of Hawthorne, just a mile south of Bristow Farms. I swiped my card, and the attendant handed me a sheet of paper with the door code for my designated showering room. I punched in the code, and the red light on the handle turned green. The shower room was ten feet wide by thirty feet long. Besides the shower, there was a toilet, a bench, and a sink. Plenty of room I thought as I turned on the two-headed showers.

I was filthy from head to toe and absolutely exhausted. I let the shower wash me away. I hoped it would provide me with a second wind. It was Friday night, and I had plans to go out in Gainesville with my cousins. I could barely stand up straight, but plenty of time for rest when I'm dead I concluded. It felt like that might be tomorrow.

I had only been in Hawthorne for just over twenty-four hours, and yet somehow, I felt as though I had never left. I was physically exhausted, but even more so, I felt emotionally exhausted. It was as though I had relived two years of my childhood in one day. The hardest two years. As I scrubbed the dirt from my skin, my hand ran over an old reminder that no matter how far or how long I left for, a part of me would always be here.

I examined the scar for the first time in years. It was barely noticeable. I had so many larger scars, and perhaps even bigger stories now. I tried to remember if my ex-wife had ever even noticed this scar. Had I even mentioned it to her? Probably not. I had tried to forget it. Why had I tried to forget it?

After I had dried and dressed, I took a seat on the bench next to the sink. I pulled up the FaceBook app on my smartphone. I entered into messenger and typed out T I N A. My sister's page popped up when I tapped her icon. I noticed that she was now living in Ocala, which was thirty miles south of Hawthorne. I chuckled, Tina believed that thirty miles were far enough, and Misty didn't believe that three thousand miles were far enough away. I sent Tina a quick message to let her know that I was in town, and would love to meet her for lunch this weekend if she had time.

I knew she had recently had her fifth child. I imagined how busy she must be keeping track of all of them. Our grandmother had six children, and I told Tina she only had two to go to win. Her scoffed response could have meant challenge accepted, or shut up. I felt like I needed to see Tina. I needed to see her children. I needed to see that this was real, and that she had in fact, survived.

13

Bound to the Farm

Bound to the Farm
1994

It turned out that doctor Laura, and I were not thinking the same thing. She arranged for Misty and Tina to complete a sleep study at the hospital that weekend. Laura's thought was that the girls would be wired up, and she would be able to document any sleep disruptions. It would be hard science which revealed this mystery.

It was a two-night study. Misty and Tina did not seem scared at all. They appeared to be excited. Their only concern was leaving Ernestine alone. They calmed down when they realized that they would be coming home during the day. They could check on Ernestine then.

The first night they were given their typical dosage of medication. Wires were stuck to their heads and their hearts. As it was described to me, I am not sure how anyone could sleep under those conditions. However, my sisters slept so hard that night that the nurses finally decided to wake them up at nine the next morning. The results showed typical, albeit deep, sleep patterns for children their ages.

My grandmother and I were shocked by the results. Neither of us could recall the last time that the girls had slept through the night. The doctor described it as a peaceful sleep. A couple of short dreams each, neither of which were a bother. Looking at Misty and Tina, they appeared completely refreshed. It wasn't just the way that they looked either. They were friendly for the first time that I could remember in a long time. They seemed happy to see me. We spent the entire car ride home chatting up a storm as if we hadn't spoken in months. In reality, we had not.

When we got home, Ernestine was sitting on the front steps and Gene was in the front yard. Gene was the mysterious black cat that had been reincarnated with Ernestine. Of course, the girls didn't know that. They named him Gene because he preferred spending most of his time in the woods, just like our Granddaddy. He hated to be indoors. Gene didn't give me the sass that Ernestine did, but I always felt as though he were watching me, just waiting. Waiting for what, I do not know. The girls scooped up Ernestine and disappeared into their bedroom. I guess the good sleep hadn't helped them that much.

That evening, when Grandma returned the girls to the hospital for their second assessment, I stayed home. I watched the white mini-van turn on to washed-out road with Ernestine. I left her sitting on the stairs, and went back into the front porch. I sat on the floor pushing a couple of toy cars around, and wishing I had someone to play with.

When I saw Ernestine make her way down the stairs, it caught my interest. I jumped to my feet and walked to the screen. Gene joined Ernestine from the wood line, and together they took their time crossing the field heading straight for the portentous farmhouse. I watched them until I couldn't see them anymore. What would be the point of following them, I thought. I felt called. "Oh God, don't start that crap," I said to myself.

Ernestine and Gene both hopped through the south window from the ground in a single bound. My hiding spot behind the bales of hay was gone. I opted for the pecan tree instead. I peeked from behind the tree hoping to see the cat through the front door. I was surprised that the front door, which had been gone for as long as I could remember, was not only hanged but also closed.

Intrigue led me back onto the porch of the farmhouse and made me forget about the cats for a moment. I tried to open the door, but it was locked. I stepped back onto the porch, and looked around, trying to make sense of the door. I didn't think that this was the house. Someone else had put the door up, but why? I looked into the house through the broken window. Nothing else looked any different. It was the same disaster it had always been. A movement high in the kitchen caught my attention. It was Ernestine, and she was lying on the high beam that still read *come home.* She was looking dead ahead, and not paying any attention to me.

I climbed into the house thru the broken window, being careful not to cut myself on any glass that remained in the sill. The window was low, and there were crates stacked along the inside wall, which made the maneuver easy, but not quiet. Ernestine glanced down, only briefly, as if to acknowledge my arrival. One reason we had always stayed out of the house was because that we either thought or had been told, that it was a snake nest. I could not see any floor in the entire living room. Plenty of hiding places for snakes. However, knowing that there were cats in the house made me feel safer.

For the first time, I began rummaging through the junk. I'm not sure if I was just bored, or if I were looking for a clue. I did not understand how this house became a dump. It wasn't just filled with junk, but trash littered the floors from wall to wall. I picked up a piece of paper, and read the faded type. It was a solicitation mailed in 1961. I found a gas bill from 1989. No one had lived in this house in 1989, I thought, and it did not even have gas lines.

It became a game. I picked up envelope after envelope checking the contents for dates. The latest correspondence I found was 1989, but the earliest envelope I picked up was postdated 1944, and it had US Army markings on it. I knew that most of my great uncles had served in the military, but 1944 would have been before their service I thought. There was no letter in the envelope, and it was only addressed to Bristow.

I picked up another ancient looking envelope. It was brittle and felt as though it might fall apart from my touch. It was difficult to tell the original color of the paper, but it was completely brown now from apparent water stains. As I turned it over and over in my hands looking for markings, I realized that the envelope was warm. It felt like it could erupt into flames any second. I looked around the room and tried to imagine how long it might take the house to burn to the ground. Minutes I thought.

There were no markings on the envelope. I was about to throw it back on the ground when I realized that there was something inside of it. I tried to lift the flap but discovered that it was sealed shut. It occurred to me that this envelope had never been opened. I was mesmerized. The possibilities were endless. I could be holding anything in my hands. There could be a check inside for one hundred dollars for all I knew. I smiled.

I tried to carefully open the envelope. For something so frail, it was sealed shut for eternity. I wondered if it were still sealed because no one could open it. I decided that if it were that important, it would not have been trashed in this house for God knows how long. I ripped off the end of the envelope, trying not to destroy whatever was inside of it.

The second that the envelope was open, a strong cold wind moved through the house, and the front door was flung open making a bang as the door hit the wall. The wind and the noise startled me so that I jumped, and dropped the envelope. The wind did not stop, and although it was late spring, it was frigid enough to make me shudder. It was not a breeze that came and went. The wind was constant, and consistently banging the door loudly against the front of the house.

I bent over to retrieve the envelope that I had dropped. It was obvious that it contained something of importance. Something that the house or the cat didn't want me to see. I was frightened, but then I thought, what else was new. A little wind would not stop me from solving this mystery. I was breathing heavily now as if I had been sprinting. I picked up the envelope and realized that, although it was May, I could see my breath.

The rickety house creaked and groaned from the wind which caused me to take pause, and slowly stand up. My attention was on the house now more than the envelope that I held in my hand. It sounded as though it were trying to speak to me, but I just could not make out what it was saying.

When I popped the envelope open to see its contents, Ernestine dropped down right onto my back and made a terrible hiss. She did not claw me and immediately pounced onto the rusted-out wood burning stove as if nothing had just happened. She sat staring at me, and I stood staring at her, waiting for her next move. It occurred to me that since she had not scratched me, perhaps she didn't want to hurt me. Maybe she just wanted to scare me. Or, as difficult as it was to fathom, maybe she was trying to warn me. Although there was a storm strength wind moving through the house, I noticed that Ernestine's fur was not blowing at all. In the midst of all of this, I suddenly wondered where Gene was?

Keeping my eye on Ernestine, I slowly emptied the contents of the envelope into my hand. As I looked down to finally see what it was in the envelope that was so important, I was once again distracted, this time by a scream. "Get out! Get out! Get out!" it wailed so loudly that I was forced to cover my ears.

I looked back to the stove for Ernestine. She was gone. As soon as I realized the cat's disappearance, the lady appeared. For the first time, I got a good look at her, up close, and a little too personal. The wind howled. Someone or something was wailing *get out*. And not five feet from me was something which I was sure could not exist, should not exist, and she was looking right through me.

She was translucent. I could see her, but I could also see the stove behind her. She wasn't much taller than I was. I realized that she was not towering over me so much, but I also could not see where she began. I didn't know if she was hovering, standing flat on the floor, or if she was reaching all of the way from hell. She seemed as though she were just as interested in me as I was in her, as she stood staring at me silently. Or maybe the wailing was her, although it did not seem to be coming from her mouth as I might expect. No, she wasn't interested in me, she was waiting for something.

She was beautiful, but in an unexpected manner. She was dressed in rags. Her vintage dress was ratty and had patches, and her hair was straight, although it did not look straightened. Her face was remarkably plain, and yet naturally stunning. It occurred to me that she looked very sad. In all of the chaos which were occurring in the house, she held an absolutely calm demeanor, and her hands were clasped together in front of her.

By the time I understood what was happening she was less than a foot away from me. Startled, I jumped back. She kept moving towards me slowly but certainly. I took one more step backward and was met with a loud screech. I looked down while jumping in the air, and saw Gene dashing into the living room. I had stepped on his tail. I quickly returned my focus to the ghost who was pursuing me.

She was no longer in front of me. She was everywhere. Beside me. On top of me. Under me. She was coming at me from all angles now. There would be no escape I thought as I scrambled backward. Surely, she was behind me too. I fell through the front door frame onto the porch. The door slammed behind me.

On the front porch, it was warm and quiet. I sat there in near tears for a moment until I realized something. I still had it. I was holding the contents of the envelope in my hand. I brought the small piece of paper to a rest between my knees, and my eyes while still sitting on the porch.

The item was as frail as the envelope, and I was surprised that it had not been destroyed by the wind or my grip. It was a photograph. Possibly a daguerreotype. It was black and white but had been turned nearly completely brown by the years, and the environment. In the picture, there was a tall skinny man standing to the left, a small child in the middle, and a skinny woman standing on the other side.

The couple was quite young, even I could tell in this ancient photo. The child was a toddler, perhaps three years old. Although the picture was black and white, it appeared that the toddler's hair had a reddish tint. The two adults in the photo did not have any telling features. I knew that was not true, but rather the photo was not the quality that

I was accustomed to in 1994. I studied the picture closer for anything that might make sense to me.

The family was standing on a porch in the photo. I jumped up from the porch that I was sitting on. It was the same porch. This family had lived in this house. Maybe they still lived in this house. Wait, that couldn't be right. I held the picture as close to my face as I could stand. I couldn't say for certain, but the lady in the picture could be the same lady whom I had just encountered inside.

"Tommy!" someone yelled behind me, "get down from there," the voice ordered.

I turned around and jumped down from the porch immediately. It was my Uncle Philip who was shouting commands. "Come over here boy," he hollered from the east fence line.

I did as I was told, and ran to my uncle. "I put that door up for a reason. I don't want you kids playing in there. Do you understand me? It's dangerous," he continued before I could answer him.

I looked down. Between Uncle Philip, and I was a fairly fresh cow patty. I looked back up to my uncle, "dangerous how?" I asked.

I knew better than to ask this type of question. Children on the farm were to do as they were told, and not challenge adults, ever. I half expected him to rap me one on the head. Instead, he looked like he might answer me. "What do you got there in yer hand?" Philip questioned.

Shoot I thought, why hadn't I shoved it in my back pocket? Obviously, he knew that I had been inside of the house. There was no point in trying to hide it now. I held up the picture to him, and he took it from me. "You got this from in the farmhouse?" he asked bluntly.

"Yessir," I responded, "who is it?" I figured no harm in asking.

"It is my mama and daddy. They lived in that house way back before you was born," Uncle Philip pointed to his childhood home.

That was the first thing that had made sense to me all day. I knew that Grandma was the oldest, and I assumed that the child was her. I thought I would ask Philip anyway since this was the most he had ever talked to me not yelling. "Is that Grandma?" I asked.

Uncle Philip stared at the picture for a moment, then stuffed it into his coverall chest pocket. "Stay out of that house you hear!" he scolded, and then headed off into the field without answering my question.

Should I tell him? Should I just holler it out? *Hey Philip, I just saw your mama in the farmhouse.* I bet that would get his attention. Then I wondered, *what if he knew.* Maybe that's what he meant by dangerous. Maybe he secretly knew that there was an entity in that house. I began wondering how far along a secret like that could be kept. Did Grandma know? Is that why she insisted there was nothing wrong with the house? Is that why everyone is acting like my sisters are going crazy, and refuse to even entertain the notion that something more is happening here? I returned home with more questions than answers. However, I had convinced myself of the obvious, the lady in the farmhouse was Ernestine.

I did not see Ernestine, the cat, until the next morning when my sisters got home. She was sitting on the stairs waiting. As if she knew exactly where they had gone, and when they would be home. I was shooting basketball a couple of hundred feet away when I saw the van pulling in. I didn't think much of it because I knew exactly what would happen. The girls would scoop up Ernestine, and disappear into their lair for the rest of the day. The thought saddened me. I missed my shot and chased the ball into the garden.

When I turned back around, I was surprised to see the girls dashing across the field to me playfully. They stopped and each picked a dandelion, then began running again, hoping that the wind would blow the flowers away. I met them just under the basketball goal. Normally, I would ask Tina if she wanted to play, but I knew if I did, that I would lose Misty because she hated basketball. "What's up?" I asked with an upbeat tone that had a hint of worry.

"Wanna play alligator?" Misty asked.

Boy did I ever. We had not played any game since last summer. I was so excited that I went easy on them. I let Tina tag me if she got stuck in the river for more than three rounds. I intentionally missed tagging Misty several times that I could have easily. We were having fun. For a few minutes, we were kids again.

That evening I learned from sneakily listening to Grandma's report to my Uncle Mark. The doctors had not given the girls their medication on the second night in the hospital. The doctors intentionally wanted to see how they would react when not medicated. They even had straps added to the beds in anticipation of the reported events, so that they could tie them down if they needed too. Imagine everyone's surprise when both girls slept soundly through the night. I was not surprised. Apparently, neither was Dr. Laura. But we had very different ideas of why.

For the first time, a thought occurred to me. Whatever has controlling my sisters, was bound to the farm.

2020

I didn't stay out late Friday night, but I did stay in Gainesville. When we called it a night, I took up my cousin Steve's offer to crash on his couch. I wasn't drunk. I could have easily driven back to the farm. I knew that I had another full days' worth of work ahead of me, and I thought that I could sleep better on some cushioning. I wondered if I was partially afraid of spending the night on the farm alone again after waking up under the pecan tree with my sister's blanket. I still could not figure out where the blanket had come from. I could only hope that I had stumbled into the trailer, and found it during my inebriation.

I slept much better and was on my way back to the farm by sunrise. Uncle Ray was already at the trailer when I arrived, which did not surprise me. He was beating on the back wall of the back porch, which would be today's objective. The back was much more solid than the front porch, and we both knew that we had our days' work cut out for us.

Ray looked like he was already whupped when I joined him. Although it was a cool morning, his shirt was already saturated in sweat. "We oughta get Philip's big tractor, and push this thing right on over," he suggested.

I laughed, "good morning to you too."

It wasn't a terrible idea except I figured it would be nearly impossible to get the tractor back there because it was so overgrown. What was once a nice open backyard, was now covered with medium-sized trees.

Mostly oak. The honeysuckle bush that I took my sugar from as a child was long gone. A small fig tree that once produced figs by the pound, had grown bigger than the house and taken over a large portion of the yard. I looked around, but could not find any indication of figs on the ground.

"Oh, you will get a kick out of this. When I came back here earlier, there was a white cat sitting on the porch there," Ray pointed to the exit from the back porch with a small chuckle.

I realized that I must not have been as awake as I thought I was, "say what?" I asked incredulously.

"Sure was. Remember that white kitten we gave the girls when ya'll was children? Might've been the same cat," Ray suggested.

I looked around frantically. I had to see the cat for myself. "That's impossible, it would be twenty-seven years old," I said aloud, but I was talking to myself more than Uncle Ray.

"Yeah, I guess yer right," Ray conceded.

"Did you see where it went?" I begged Ray.

"Oh, it was obviously feral. It had a big scar running along its side. It hissed at me, and ran off into the woods," Ray explained.

"A scar...that's impossible," I said softly to myself.

14

Gene is the Monster

Gene is the Monster
1994

Misty and Tina were completely refreshed and returned to the girls of old. They were children again it seemed. We played the entire day, and they didn't once pay any attention to Ernestine. After an early lunch, the girls suggested that we go play in the creek. I warned them that it was still low because, although they might not have realized it, we had not had much rain in weeks.

Sure as shootin, there wasn't even enough water running thru the creek to stand in. It was such a small trickle that I could not even see its trademark red tint. By early afternoon, it was sweltering and humid. The farm was begging the sky to rain. I knew that it was too hot to go inside, but I was afraid that our misery would drive the girls to their cave; and Ernestine. A thought hit me like a bolt of lightning: maybe Ernestine knew it was too hot to be inside too.

Misty stated the obvious aloud first, "gosh it's freakin hot!"

"No kidding," I didn't mean it sarcastically, "maybe we could go play with the water hose," I suggested.

Tina looked toward the hot box, "naw, I bet Granddaddy is sittin on the porch. He will just yell at us to quit wastin' water," she was right.

Then, Tina did the last thing I would have ever expected. She stood facing the wooded swamp quietly for a few seconds, then piped up, "I bet that water hole we found back there has water in it."

Misty and I looked at each other in disbelief. Well, my look was disbelief, I can't really speak to what Misty may have been thinking, but her mouth was as wide open as mine.

"Surely you can't be serious," I made more of a statement than a question.

"What?" Tina pointed down the fence line, "the fence isn't overgrown yet, we wouldn't have to go into the pasture, or the woods."

I looked across the short field to the fence. What she said made sense, but still didn't feel right. "What about your monster?" I asked trying not to mock.

Tina looked to the wooded swamp once more, then glanced back at the shed as though she were hatching a plan. "I'm not scared anymore. Plus, we can take weapons with us this time," she said pointing to the dilapidated shed.

I was never one to turn down an adventure. As hot as it was, that water hole under the shaded pines sounded mighty nice. What kept replaying in my mind were Tina's words, *I'm not scared anymore.* I couldn't help, but wonder what had changed. This day suddenly felt strange, but I would not trade strange for boredom. Misty kept quiet during this debate and seemed content to go along with whatever was decided. Stranger and stranger.

We each picked a weapon from the tool shed. I chose a sling blade. It had a handle that was twice as long as an axe, and on one end was a twelve-inch thin steel blade that was kept razor sharp. It was perfect for clearing thickets, but I was unsure of what else it might be good for. Either way, I felt powerful as I held the tool like a staff, with the blade beginning at eye level. Tina found a worthless machete. The blade was so rusted that I thought that it might snap if she actually tried to cut anything with it, but it was the perfect size for her and made her feel safe. Misty chose the oddest tool. She picked up a three-pronged pitch-fork that was probably older than all of us combined. The metal looked loosely attached to the handle, and it was entirely covered with rust. If she stabbed anything, and only wounded it, it would certainly die from tetanus. If we had to run, she would have to drop the pitchfork because it was far too large for her to handle properly.

As we approached the fence we slowed to a halt. We wouldn't have to search for or wonder where Sam was this time. We all had him dead in our sights. Sam was lying under a small patch of shade trees resting from the day's heat. Fortunately, he was not looking in our direction. I turned to the girls, "Ok, same as last time. It doesn't matter that we are on this side of the fence. If we run, Sam runs. Keep low and slow. If he sees us and comes, move into the trees and either get behind one or climb it. Do not, under any circumstances, lose sight of each other," I ended my instructions, for what they were worth.

We moved as slowly and quietly as possible down the fence line. Al-though it was not as nearly overgrown as it would be by midsummer, like it had been last year, it was growing quickly. The lack of rain had probably slowed the growth. Regardless, we had to hack our way through several thick areas. I would cut while Misty and Tina kept their eye on Sam. I wondered how difficult it would be to make and maintain a permanent path through here to access the water hole all summer.

It took longer than I expected, but we made it. I didn't expect the water hole to be as deep as it had been the previous summer since it had not begun raining yet. I was somehow wrong. The water hole appeared to be just as deep as it had been last summer, and it looked to be even bigger. It did not make sense, but we did not care. Within seconds we were all stripped down to our underwear, and splashing in the water.

The water was almost cold. At first, it was a shock, but that quickly turned into a feeling of complete refreshment. It was also tempting to take a drink. This school year, I had started middle school. I was in the sixth grade at Hawthorne Jr. and Sr. High School. Just a few weeks ago we had learned about Florida spring water. I knew that springs, large and small, all over Florida, popped up from Florida's underground aquifer. The water temperature ranged from sixty-eight to seventy degrees year-round. I was now certain that we had found a small spring on Bristow Farms.

There was still a major discrepancy which I could not explain. Florida spring water is world-renowned for its crystal-clear cleanliness. We learned that the environmental protection agency (EPA), even deemed Florida spring water is safe to drink. If all of that were true, and this was a spring, then why was the water red?

I wanted to enjoy the first water play of the year with my sisters. Then I thought, I wanted to enjoy the first play, period, of the year with my sisters. But the red water was a curiosity that my mind could not evade. There was absolutely no visible reason that this water should be red.

As one thought led to another, I was reminded of the nearby bone pile. There were simply too many mysteries here for one boy to solve. I wondered if the bone pile was still there. That's silly I thought, of course it is still there. Who would have moved it? The real question is, why is it there? Who put it there?

As I sat enjoying the cool water, I stared in the direction that the bone pile was in. The most rational explanation I could come up with was coyotes. I had never actually seen a coyote on the farm, but at night I could hear them howling in the woods. It made sense that one animal could not have done this. Yes, it must be a pack of coyotes.

The hole in my logic was that coyotes do not come out during the day much. The thought made me feel safer for a moment. I considered that perhaps a pack coyotes had made the wooded swamp their den. No one ever came back here. It was completely plausible I thought. When I entered their den, it scared them. However, I couldn't imagine that coyotes liked to swim. The splash that we heard would have to be the biggest coyote ever.

I climbed out of the water hole and picked up my blade on a stick. "Where are you going?" my sisters stopped giggling.

"Ya'll just keep playing here. I want to see if the bone pile is still there," I informed the girls.

They happily obliged and went back to playing in the water, leaving me to my own devices. I slowly and cautiously crept toward the swamp. If there was a pack of coyotes in there, then it was obvious that they wanted nothing to do with me. They had plenty of opportunity to attack by now. No, they just wanted to be left alone. Except this pile of bones indicated otherwise.

Sure enough, the pile was still there. I could not tell if it were much bigger, although I had expected it to be. I picked up bone after bone examining each closely. None of the bones seems to have chew marks on them. They had been picked clean. One thing that I knew about dogs, is that they loved to chew on bones. It just was not adding up for me.

Then I saw the cow skull that I assumed was the same one Misty had held the year before. I picked it up. I ran my hands over it. There was a deep groove in the bone that ran from above the eye socket all the way down past where the cow's snout would have been. This was not a chew mark either. I remembered the bear from the big oak that John had shot. A story was forming in my mind, and it was not nearly as scary as I imagined it would be.

Things were making sense to me now. At least about the bone pile. I felt a sense of accomplishment as if I had solved a riddle. I smiled to myself and looked over at my sisters still splashing in the water hole. I can figure this all out I thought. I picked up what must have a vertebrae bone, and tossed it into the air a few times, catching it as it fell. I turned back to the swamp that had nothing to say and laughed at it. I wound up a tight pitch, and tossed the vertebrae deep into the swamp, and watched it splash into the black water.

As I watched the water ripple out, I caught sight of something I hadn't noticed before. Hunkered down on the other side of the body of black water was another black body, with green eyes. I took a cautious step backward, and the black body stood up to attack. "Ruunnnnnn!!" I screamed to my sisters as I turned, and opened into a full sprint.

I still had the blade in my hand, but dropped it as I realized its uselessness, and that it was slowing me down. I heard splashing behind me, letting me know that the monster was in pursuit. Misty and Tina were already out of the water hole by the time I reached it, and I joined them in a dash to the fence line. There was no chance for debate this time, we would have to run with the bull. I watched the barbed wire ahead of us explode, and disappear behind a wall of white.

There was no escape. Sam was running right for us, and he was already less than fifty feet away by the time we realized it. I wrapped my arms around my sisters and tackled them to the ground. As my head dropped, the last thing that I saw was Sam charging, which his head down, and enormous horns coming right for us.

The next sensation I felt was shock. I heard bone crunching bone, but I felt nothing. Sam was past us now, but I was scared to look back. I was certain he would have one of my sisters on each of his enormous horns. Then I realized that Misty and Tina were lying beside me. I looked back just in time to see Sam toss a large black cat into the water.

Stunned by what my eyes were seeing, I realized that we had a chance to escape. I pulled my sisters up from the ground, and pushed them toward the pasture, "Run," I encouraged them unnecessarily.

We all ran past the fence, and into the pasture, "keep going, don't stop until you get home," these were marching orders because I had stopped.

I had to see this battle. I hid behind a large oak tree to watch Sam take on what I had finally identified as a black panther. The panther had not retreated into the swamp from Sam's rude arrival. He was on his hind legs swiping in the air and growling at Sam. The panther was massive. On two legs, from where I stood, he looked every bit as big as Sam the bull. Sam was not about to back down either. He was pushing the dirt with his hoof furiously preparing for his next charge at the large cat.

As soon as the panther fell back onto all four feet Sam charged with determination. The cat did not run away and did not appear to be scared at all. The panther moved towards Sam with far greater agility, and as Sam missed his target, the panther ripped open Sam's side from his shoulder all the way to his back leg.

Sam let out a cry that I could not have expected and went down hard sliding across the bank of the water hole. The cat tumbled too from the sheer weight of the bull, but never lost his footing. The panther stopped himself with a tree, by bounding up it seven or eight feet, and then pouncing off back to the ground to prepare for his next attack.

Sam was back on his feet, but not prepared to charge as the panther came flying at him again, this time head-on. Sam turned his head at the last second in anticipation of the cat's full weight, and razor-sharp claws. There was a loud growl as I slapped my hands over my eyes. I wanted to see but I couldn't watch.

Seconds passed of wincing cries from both animals. I finally opened my fingers enough to peek out in hopes of figuring out what had happened. Both animals were piled up together motionless. I stepped out from behind the tree, and watched silently for at least five minutes, expecting something to happen. Finally, from a distance, I heard Misty yell, "Tommy, come on."

I looked east toward the creek and pond and saw both sisters standing just on the pasture side of the fence. They were ok, and they knew that I was ok. I looked back toward the bull and the panther. I took a few steps toward them, stopped, and then a few steps more. I reached down and found Tina's machete, and picked it up. I threw it at the beasts and watched as it bounced off, and sink in the water hole. Neither animal moved or made a sound.

Both animals were dead. As I got closer, I could see Sam's intestines flowing from his stomach into the water hole. The water was dark red. I nearly threw up at the sight. I moved to the other side partially to block my view of the disgusting scene, and partly because I wanted to see what had happened to the panther.

Just as only a few minutes before, which felt like a lifetime ago, I saw his eyes first. The panther's eyes were bright green, and although he was certainly dead, they seemed to shine brighter now than they had in the swamp. I could not see his blood against his magnificent black fur, but he looked very wet as if water were pouring from his skin. Sam had gored the panther, right through his belly. Sam's horn was stuck all of the way through the panther by half of a foot.

I gathered up our clothes, and the tools, and trudged back to my sisters carrying all of it. I found them kicking around in the creek trickle, obviously waiting for me. By my sitting tree, next to the creek, I dropped everything that I was carrying and collapsed. Misty finally asked, "what happened?"

I sighed loudly and stood up slowly facing my sisters. I turned slightly to Tina, and dropped my dirty hands onto her tiny shoulders, "Sam killed your monster."

That was all that was said. It was almost as if the girls somehow knew. Knew that my report was true. They didn't even question what the monster was. We put the tools away and retreated back to the safety of the front yard. Some fools never learn, I thought of myself.

The next morning before school, just as the sun was rising, a familiar pick-up truck pulled into the front yard. My heart skipped a beat at what that meant. It was Uncle Philip. He had found Sam. I listened closely as he described the event to my grandparents. "For the last couple of years, I have been losing cows, and couldn't explain it. I knew it wasn't coyotes because they aren't capable of dragging off an entire carcass. I thought maybe it might've been that bear that John killed last summer, but the cows kept disappearing. This morning I found one of my bulls back in the swamp, opened up from head to tail. It was a panther that killed my cows," Philip stated matter-of-factly.

Grandma and Granddaddy looked at each other in shock. We had seen bears, bobcats, and even foxes on the farm, but never a panther. "How do you know it was a panther?" Granddaddy inquired.

"Because the bull ran it right though. Gored him. The panther is still laying back there stuck on his horn," Philip said with a smidgen of pride.

I looked to my sisters who had heard the entire story. We knew the rest of the tale, but we wouldn't tell. Sam was a hero. He had saved us. He might have saved a bunch more cattle too it sounded like. I thought that maybe that is why Sam was so protective of the pasture. Maybe he didn't have an anger issue after all. Maybe he was just protecting his herd.

Before school, for the first time since they had returned home from the hospital the day before, the girls mentioned Ernestine. I was shocked to learn that the cat had not spent the night in the girl's bedroom. Tina noticed that Ernestine was not sitting on the doorsteps as we left for school. "Well, it sounds to me that you guys have learned to live without each other every second of the day. Not a bad thing," I offered.

That was all that was said until we got home that evening, and Ernestine was nowhere to be found. After much discussion, the girls wanted to go check the farmhouse. I could not convince them that it was a bad idea, but I did prove to them that Uncle Philip had locked the house up, and told us to stay out of it. "She will come home when she is ready," I assured the girls.

Ernestine was gone for weeks. The girls were not nearly as upset as I imagined that they would be. By the third week, it appeared that perhaps Ernestine was gone for good. Things were back to normal, and my sister's room had even started to air out. School was over, and summer had begun, but this summer would be very different than the last. That might not be a bad thing.

Ernestine reappeared one morning as we were departing the farm. We were leaving to go to my mother's house in Gainesville for the day. When the girls spotted Ernestine coming across the field, they begged Grandma to stop the van. They jumped out, and Ernestine came right up to them as if she had never left. I got out of the van too, surprised that the cat was back. While the girls were stroking her fur hard enough to pull it out, I noticed something. Ernestine had a new scar running down her side, from her shoulder to her tail. It finally occurred to me that perhaps Ernestine was here to protect her herd too. We never saw Gene again.

2020

Uncle Ray once again worked me like he owned me, and by 4 p.m. I was nearly a broken man. As expected, the backroom was far sturdier than the front porch had been. Every beam and stud were double plated and reinforced. Having no electricity made the job that much more burdensome. I had one chainsaw and had broken all of my chains during the day. We could not cut it, we could not push it, nor could we pull the building down. Our efforts felt futile.

Ray had called Uncle Philip around noon to ask if we could use his big tractor to take the back room of Grandma's house down. He was certain that the big John Deere tractor would make light work of the job. Unfortunately, the tractor was being used for farm work, and we could not have access to it until maybe the evening, or the following morning. Because I was on a tight timeline, I felt like we had no choice but to keep doing the best we could with our own backs and the small Ford tractor.

It was nearly 4:30 p.m. when we finally decided to call it quits. We had given it our best, and yet the room still looked mostly intact, and mocked us. A short rain had moved across Bristow Farms, and left us with a welcomed cool breeze. "We should have rested during the heat of the day, it may have gone better in the cool evening," I stated obnoxiously to my uncle.

I had served a successful military career on a foundational philosophy that my grandmother had engrained into every fiber of my being. She had taught me from before I could remember that *you aren't done until the job is done*. Now, here I sat defeated on my own land, by my own hand.

It was too late now, and we both knew it. We were spent. I was sitting under the open carport, hanging my head in either exhaustion or defeat, when Ray jumped to his feet. My immediate thought was, *no way, Uncle Ray had gotten another wind, I cannot do anymore today*. I was thankful when Ray did not look to the backroom but instead fixed his gaze across the field. "What's wrong," I asked.

"I thought I heard a tractor coming," he said, walking away from the house.

As I slowly stood up, like an eighty-year-old man, I saw what Ray had heard. Coming across the field slowly, looking larger than life, in true hero fashion, was an enormous John Deere green tractor. Ray and I looked at each other and weakly cheered. By the time Philip and his tractor reached us, we realized that while it was a miracle, it also meant that we were not done for the day.

The rain had stopped baling production, Philip informed us. It was apparent that he was not impressed with our progress on the back room. "Have ya'll just been sitting up here all day waiting on me?" Uncle Philip asked sarcastically.

Neither Ray nor I could barely feign a chuckle much less a retort. The first thing that we realized was that Uncle Ray was right, the John Deere would not fit in the back yard because there were so many overgrown trees. Ray and I were investigating solutions when Philip shouted down from his high throne on the tractor, "just hook the chain around that tree, and I will yank it out."

That tree was a solid, beautiful, thirty-foot tall magnolia tree. My grandmother's favorite variety of tree. I remembered planting one in the front yard, and this one in the back yard, as a child. The thought of ripping out this history made me sad. I was skeptical that the tractor could pull it, but the only other choice was the nearby one-hundred-foot oak tree, and I knew that would be impossible.

Once the chain was hooked around the base of the tree, and the tractor, we backed up and waited to see what would happen. I expected it to take a few yanks, and be a struggle, even for this tractor with ten-foot tires. Philip didn't try to gun the tractor. He simply drove forward, as slow as the tractor could possibly go. Ray and I were forced into shock as the tree peeled out of the ground without a fight. The John Deere did not struggle in the slightest. In an instant, thirty-years of nature and nurture were both defeated by a machine, without a bead of sweat, or a single tear.

The tree was pulled out with such ease, that I was certain that the backroom would pull down, and out just as easily. Our major regret was that we had cut the large room in so many places. The best that we could hope for, was that it would pull apart in sections, and not just crumble.

It was as we feared. There was nowhere left to get a good hook on what was left of the frame to pull it out. We were exasperated and exhausted. I looked up to Philip sitting in the air-conditioned cab of the tractor, and he opened the door. "Thanks for coming up and offering to help, but I think that we have destroyed the porch beyond the capability of pulling it," I explained.

Uncle Philip looked at the sad structure for a moment, and then back to me. "That's ok, I can just push it down, and around to the fire," he stated as though I should have realized it.

I didn't know how to respond. At this point, I just wanted to be done for the day. I knew that no matter what, the John Deere was the key to destroying this monstrosity without killing ourselves in the process. I wasn't sure that what Philip suggested was possible, but I offered him his best shot and moved out of his way.

The front loader of the John Deere raised up higher than I would have thought possible and towered above the roof of the back room. The bucket tilted forward and lowered onto the roof. I half expected the building to stand resilient, and mock the John Deere as it had us for the entire day. Instead, the roof and walls chose to ridicule us by collapsing effortlessly under the power of the big green machine. Ray and I looked at each other in disbelief.

Uncle Philip and his workhorse had accomplished in ten minutes more than Uncle Ray, and I had in ten hours. My grandma used to say that *you have to use the proper tools to properly complete a job.* There was plenty of small debris left to pick up in the backyard, but that could wait for another time. For now, I only wanted to sit with my uncles and watch this piece of the hotbox burn one last time.

I told Uncle Philip that the first thing I would do once I moved back, was buy a tractor just like his. The John Deere was certainly capable of anything; I was sure of it. I thanked Philip repeatedly. I was so impressed with what I had just witnessed that I could not stop talking about it.

Uncle Philip just chuckled, "yeah, you should have seen me push down that big farmhouse up by the pecan tree."

I tried to imagine the two-story wooden house tipping over on its side. Another casualty of progress. I wondered if it would still be standing if not for the John Deere. Surely the only reason it stood for so long was that no one had the energy to tear it down. Then the realization hit.

"Did you say that you pushed down the old farmhouse?" I pointed the question to Philip.

"Oh yeah, almost twenty years ago now. I just put the bucket under the edge of the house and lifted it until it fell over, away from the pecan trees. Then I pushed it into a pile like this and set it ablaze. Shoot, I bet the entire house was gone in less than fifteen minutes. It burned so fast," Philip paused his story.

"Wow! Grandma told me that a storm blew that house down," I informed my uncles.

Uncle Philip looked at Uncle Ray, "yeah, well, you know how she is. Theresa would have been mad as a hornet. She might come back and haunt you for tearing down this trailer," he chuckled, "she never would have forgiven me for demolishing her childhood home. But it was my home too. I hated to do it, but it had to go. Yeah, I told her that a storm blew it down."

I immediately knew that Uncle Philip was right. He was right about the farmhouse, and about the trailer. She never would have left it to me had she thought that I would destroy it so soon. The trailer was unlivable just as the farmhouse was unlivable. But something about the way Philip said *but it had to go*, forced me to ask one more time.

"Makes sense," I chuckled halfheartedly, "but why did it have to go?" I asked hoping for a truthful answer after all of these years.

Philip was still sitting up on his tractor, but now he looked away from me. He stared at the fire for an uncomfortable moment, as if he were recalling something from long ago; something unpleasant. Finally, he responded with similar words which he had once already told me nearly thirty years before, "the house was dangerous."

15

Three Birthday's and a
Mistake

The summer of my thirteenth birthday began two days before school actually let out for the year. I felt special getting to end the school year early, and for a good reason. I had my first full-time job.

Last summer, and occasionally throughout the year, I had helped my uncles with their businesses. One uncle operated his own lawn service and another offered fence installation. When lawn service slowed down in the winter, they focused their efforts on fencing jobs. It wasn't as hard as it sounded, because winters in Florida are relatively short. For me, it put a little cash in my pocket and helped me feel less inferior than my friends, whom I assumed always had money.

The summer of '95 was the most time I had spent away from Bristow farms in my entire life. I walked out of the front door at 6:30 a.m., and got back to the farm around 7 p.m. every day. Most days were spent mowing commercial properties, or city folks' lawns. At such a young age, it was difficult for me to understand why strangers would pay others to mow their own lawn. Depending on how much we got accomplished each day, I made between twenty, and forty dollars a day. It wasn't all about money for me. I also got to eat out for lunch most days, which was an entirely new experience for me, I got all of the diet Pepsi I could want to drink, and I learned the value of efficiency.

I was pretty good at saving my money, but then again what could I spend it on? I was saving for two specific reasons: 1. I was determined to own a mountain bike, although there are no mountains on Bristow Farms. 2. I was begging my grandparents to let me attend a large international camporee in Oshkosh, Wisconsin at the end of summer. The primary deterrent was the $1000 registration fee, plus food, and some gear that I wanted. My sisters and I attended the Florida camporee in the Spring, and I particularly enjoyed camping and improving my scouting with new friends. I made a deal with my grandmother that if I could save the money, she would let me go.

Farm work reduced significantly that summer. My grandfather became quite ill and was incapable of doing anything for himself other than complaining. My grandmother had to stop working almost completely. She did not get much sleep at night because that is when he needed the most attention. As a result, we only planted a small garden for the family that summer, which for the most part, my sisters could manage. I cut the fields on the weekend, which wasn't nearly as fun now that I spent the entire week mowing.

My sisters and I had always been fairly self-sufficient, but now we had to be completely self-reliant. We made all of our own meals, did our own laundry, and cleaned after ourselves and grandparents entirely. The only times I really saw our grandparents were to help pick up and move Granddaddy; usually multiple times during the middle of the night.

I wasn't your typical thirteen-year-old by modern means. I was already taller than six feet and towered over my grandparents, and uncles by a good six inches. Solidified by years of hard labor, I felt confident to tackle any task. I was young and motivated, and my size helped me to accomplish more than most boys my age.

My sisters were not typical tweens either. More than the hard work they had endured during their young lives, was the hardship of synthesizing the unnatural phenomenon which they bore yet no one was likely to believe. Were they crazy or was something really happening at Bristow Farms?

June flew by and before we knew it, our birthday month had arrived. Birthdays never meant much around the farm. Usually, Grandma would make one cake for all of our birthdays, since they were all in July, and the birthday boy/girl would get a small gift. The present would never be something that we wanted, but rather something we needed. Not this year. This year my sisters, and I would get something that we wanted; I was determined.

Tina's birthday comes first and is early in the month. My days had been so long, that it actually snuck up on me. I finally came into the house around dusk, which was after 9 p.m. As had become usual, my grandparents were in their bedroom with the door closed. When I entered the kitchen my stomach automatically grumbled, and I immediately attacked the icebox looking for anything that appeared edible.

I was so exhausted and focused on food, that I did not notice my sisters sitting at the dining table. I assumed that this time of evening that if they weren't in front of the t.v., that they must be in their bedroom. I turned from the fridge with a large box of Velveeta cheese, content to make a sandwich when I noticed the girls patiently waiting. In front of them sat a two-tiered cake with strawberry frosting, and eleven candles ready to be lit. Even in my current state, it only took a second to register that it was Tina's birthday.

As I joined them at the table, I dropped the bread, mayonnaise, cheese, plate, and knife. "Hey! Happy birthday sis!" I gave a big toothy smile to Tina.

My words began their waves of excitement as they told me about the cake and their day. "After you finish your sandwich, can we sing *Happy Birthday?*"

I looked at the cake again, admiring the girl's work. The cake looked refreshingly delicious, but the hot box was already melting the strawberry icing which resembled what I imagined the candles would look like momentarily. I picked up the lighter from the table, and handed it to Misty, "I think that Tina has waited long enough," encouraging her to light the candles.

We sang Happy Birthday at the top of our lungs. I think that we wanted our grandparents to know that life was continuing outside of their bedroom. Maybe we also hoped they might join us. Misty cut into the cake to reveal vanilla with real strawberries mixed in. It was not difficult to read the genuine delight on Tina's face, and gradually my weariness melted away.

I never touched my sandwich. We sat at the table and ate the whole cake. We laughed and talked the entire time. We talked about nothing, and we talked about everything. The reality of our situation did not exist for this conversation. Good times were recounted and fabricated for the future. Finally, Misty leaned over from her chair and nudged me, "can we give her the presents now?" she asked.

Although her words were soft, they were also intended for Tina to hear, and she did. A look of confusion and surprise was set in her expression. "I suppose that we have just about waited as long as we can," I joked while taking my leave from the table to retrieve the gifts.

In mid-June, I had asked Misty what she wanted to get Tina for her birthday. She understood that I was making money now, and thought I was rich. "Tina wants a pony!" she exclaimed.

"Yes, I know she does, and a four-wheeler," I added, "I do too, but let's think a lot cheaper."

Misty eventually decided on a reasonable gift, and one day during lunch Uncle Mark took me to Walmart to purchase the items. As I made my way back to my bedroom to dig out the presents, I hoped that Tina was smart enough to realize that I didn't have anything that large in my closet, and also that she would not be disappointed. I returned to the dining room with two wrapped presents. I handed one to Misty and gave mine to Tina first.

Tina was giddy with excitement and held the gift for a long time inspecting the wrapping, and guessing what it might be. Finally, unable to stand the anticipation any longer I demanded that she open it, lest I return it to the store. She didn't have to be told twice and ripped thru the thin paper with a fury which could not be matched by me on my best day.

I don't think that she would have ever guessed the gift. I worried that it was partially selfish, but it was apparent immediately that she loved it. I helped her cut free the set of dual super soakers from the packaging as I imagined the water wars that we could have. She could not wait. As soon as the first gun was free, she snatched it and ran to the kitchen sink to fill it up. Within minutes there was water all over the house, and both of us were soaked, and silly with excitement. Misty ducked the battle but laughed at our shenanigans.

Once the guns were empty, and we agreed that the battle should continue outdoors, we returned to the table for Misty's gift. Tina did not waste any time opening this present. It was a Cabbage Patch doll that she had seen advertised every day on t.v. Tina wept with joy as she embraced the doll tightly to her face. She could have never imagined that she would own something from the picture box for herself.

Suddenly, Tina sat the doll on the table, and a serious, almost severe look came over her. She just sat and stared at Misty and I for a long moment. I was just about to ask what was wrong when she sprang from the chair. It looked to me as though she had just cleared the entire table in a single bound, lurching onto Misty and myself. She somehow grabbed both of our necks, wrapping her tiny arms around both of us, and squeezing with all of her might. I could feel moisture from her face, and I was pretty sure that it wasn't from the super soaker. "This is the best birthday ever!" she exclaimed.

Ten days passed quicker than a holiday, and just like that, it was Misty's birthday. Tina wanted to make Misty her favorite dessert, but neither of us had any idea how. Instead, I told Tina that I would pick up a cheesecake, Misty's favorite, and try to be home earlier in the evening to celebrate.

As soon as Tina's birthday had passed, we set out to arrange the same present surprise for Misty. Tina got her sister a different cabbage patch doll so that they could play together. At first, I thought that the idea wasn't very original, but then I realized that I had basically done the same thing with water guns. Her idea was every bit as thoughtful as my own, and would surely build some memories together.

I had a little more trouble coming up with a gift idea for Misty. Tina was still a little girl who loved to play outdoors and explore, but Misty had turned into a young woman in the last year, and our likes were quite different now. In the end, I spent far more on Misty's present than Tina's. I think it was because I felt guilty that I wasn't sure what she would like. I got her a pair of Nike running shoes. She liked running, and so I figured she would need a good pair of shoes for it. They were the first designer clothing items that any of us ever owned.

On Misty's birthday, early morning storms rolled through Bristow Farms one after another. By 11 a.m. Uncle Mark decided to stop waiting for it to clear up. He was going to take the day to go into Gainesville to shop. A day off sounded nice, and maybe I could convince Misty I had taken the day off just for her birthday. She'd never buy it.

Shortly after noon Tina came to me and asked about Misty's cheese-cake. I had planned to buy it on the way home from work. Now, Mark was gone, and Grandma was sleeping. I had bought lemon cake ingredients for my cake two days later, but I supposed that we could just use that now for Misty's cake. Tina didn't like that idea at all, and to be honest, I wasn't keen on it either.

There was one obvious solution. I just needed to go to the store and buy the cheesecake; no problem. The only grocery store in Hawthorne was Miller's Supermarket, and it was two miles south of Bristow Farms of Highway 301. There were three unused vehicles sitting in our front yard. I could just drive to Miller's, get the cheesecake, and be back in ten minutes before anyone realized the car, or I was even gone.

Tina liked the idea and wanted to come with me. I knew that if I got caught it would be bad. If I got caught with my baby sister with me, it would be worse. I convinced Tina to keep Misty distracted while I left and to be prepared to cover for me if our grandparents stirred. I just needed ten minutes.

I decided to take the hunk of junk station wagon, mainly because I figured that it probably needed to be run. It hadn't been used in over six months since my grandfather had become ill. I couldn't help but grin as I sat behind the steering wheel, and had to move the seat back. Any worry that I had melted away.

Hawthorne has never had a police department. However, Alachua County Sheriff's Office (ASo) routinely patrolled Hawthorne city limits and 301. Then, of course, there was also the Florida Highway Patrol (FHP) who loved hunting truckers trying to avoid I-75. But first, I had to get off of the farm, which meant I had to get past Aunt Tojuanna's watchful eye.

I knew that the key to this entire operation was to go slow. If Tojuanna saw the station wagon slowly pulling across the field, she would be far less likely to think anything of it than if she saw it moving quickly. I had a bad habit of driving anything that moved at its limit; whether it be a tractor, a four-wheeler, or yes even a car. But if I drove slowly, no one would ever suspect a twelve-year-old to be pulling onto US Highway 301. I would be thirteen in two days I reminded myself.

It worked. At least enough to make it to the highway. I sat at the Bristow Farms exit preparing to turn southbound for far longer than I expected. The cars passing by suddenly seemed to be moving much faster than I had ever noticed before. For a brief moment, I questioned myself: maybe I should just pull into Aunt Tojuanna's house, and ask her to take me to the store? Surely, she would. As soon as I had considered the thought, I dismissed it, I could do this, I didn't need any help.

I pulled onto 301 southbound headed for Miller's grocery store. I stayed in the slow lane and intentionally did not exceed sixty miles per hour. Several cars passed me, but I dared not look into their cabs. I was certain that they would know that I was not old enough to drive. Or, even worse, they might recognize me. As each of the cars passed, I made certain to check their license plates. Two were out of state, and two were out of county. I felt safe.

As I entered city limits, the speed limit reduced from 65 m.p.h. to 45 m.p.h. I obeyed the limit and even used my turn signal to move into the inside lane so that I could turn into Miller's. Turning into Miller's meant crossing the two lanes of northbound traffic. While the speed limit was slowed twenty miles per hour, the cars seemingly were not. Car after car zipped by. As I sat in the middle of the highway waiting to turn, at the far north end of the parking lot I spotted two ASO cruisers parked in front of the Subway restaurant. I could not tell if there was anyone in the cars, or if they were inside eating. Either way, I could feel them watching me.

After sitting in the median for about thirty minutes, or thirty seconds, I could not tell, there was a break in traffic, and I zipped across into Miller's parking lot. As I pulled to the east lot, as close to Miller's and far away from Subway as I could, I kept my eye on the police cruisers, expecting their lights to come on any second. Once I had pulled into a parking spot and turned off the engine, I accepted that I would not be arrested yet. I sat in the car trying to decide if I should wait until the cops left to go in, and do my shopping.

After seeing no movement from the vehicle for several minutes, I decided to proceed. I walked into Miller's as I had a thousand times before, but everything seemed different. The manager's smile seemed to know more. The bag boy, who was probably a year or two older than me, definitely knew that I was up to something. I breezed through the front of the store as quickly as possible, directly for the cheesecake. I picked up the first one I saw, without inspecting it at all, and made an about-face to the checkout counter.

I was almost jogging when out of an aisle came a familiar face. I barely noticed him as I tripped over his cart, and scrambled not to drop my dessert. Before I could correct myself or apologize, I heard his booming yet caring voice, "boy you better slow down before you hurt someone."

The voice was all too familiar. He was the last person I wanted to see given the situation. Pop Herring was the dean of Hawthorne Jr./Sr. High School. He was also the most well-known, and respected member of the community. He was a military veteran of the Vietnam War, and a religious leader in town as well. He would want to talk.

"What's the hurry?" Pop asked as though the store aisle were his hallway at the schoolhouse.

"Hiya Pop. My Grandma sent me in to get this cake for my sisters' birthday, but we are in a hurry on account my Granddaddy is at home sick," I tried to rationalize, and disengage.

"I'm real sorry to hear about yo daddy," Pop sympathized, "how is work going for ya?"

Pop had a way of taking the edge off of any conversation. You couldn't help but want to talk to him no matter what the situation was. "Oh, it's going real well. I have earned a lot of money. I bought my sisters some presents, and I am gonna buy a mountain bike this week, and I will have saved enough to go camping in Wisconsin in August," I told Pop proudly.

"Well now, that sounds real fine young man. You just make sure to take care of your momma too," Pop always advised me the same thing; take care of Grandma.

"Yessir," I answered losing a little of my pride.

"Where is your mamma anyway? I wanna say hello. I haven't seen her in an age," Pop asked.

Every November Pop brought us a frozen turkey to cook for Thanksgiving dinner, and as far as I knew, that was the last time he had seen, or heard from Grandma. "She is waiting for me in the car, she isn't feeling too well," I lied to Pop, and I knew he knew it.

"Ok then, you send her my best, and keep up the good work," Pop said as he turned down the next aisle.

Crisis adverted.

I climbed back into the driver's seat of the station wagon and sat the cheesecake in the passenger's seat. The cop cars had not moved, and I figured I would scoot on out before they had a chance to exit the restaurant. I backed the car out of the parking spot and shifted into drive. As the car began to roll forward, I checked my rearview mirror one last time. Standing at the crosswalk was Pop and his buggy, staring directly at the station wagon.

The short drive back to Bristow Farms seemed twice as long as the journey into town. I just knew I had been caught. Not if, but when he called my Grandma, my summer would be over, including the big camping trip which I had worked so hard, and saved so much for. Surprisingly, I felt far worse about getting caught lying to Pop, than breaking the law. He would never believe another word I said now. He would never be proud of me again either. My mind examined every worst possible scenario on the drive home.

When I pulled off of 301 entering the farm, I stopped to check the mail. It had not been checked in several days I could tell by how crammed full the box was. I managed to get everything out of the box and shut, when I turned around to the car, I spotted Uncle Mark's truck pulling in behind me. I waved to him hoping to appease any curiosity; it didn't work. He called me from his truck. I threw the mail in the car and walked back to his window.

"What are you doing?" he asked in an accusing tone.

"Just checking the mail. I don't think it's been checked in a week, seems like," I shrugged.

Mark considered my words for a moment while examining the position of the station wagon. "Alright, but don't be crossing the railroad anymore. Park on the other side and walk across," Mark commanded.

"Ok," I responded as I walked away.

The expedition created more excitement than I could ever imagine the small town having. I pulled back into the yard and was immediately greeted by Tina. I got out of the car with my hands full of mail. "Where is the cheesecake?" Tina whined.

"Shhh, it's in the front seat. Just wait for a second for Mark to go inside," I instructed her.

She looked over to Mark's house, and saw him getting out of his truck, and heading for his backdoor. She knew there was more to the story, and looked to me for an explanation. I waved the mail at her and headed onto the porch. A minute later she joined me on the porch with the cheesecake in her hands. "Should I put this in the refrigerator to keep chilled?" she asked.

I thought about it for a second, "Why wait, let's get Misty, and get this party started."

We brought plates, silverware, and Misty's presents onto the porch before calling the birthday girl out. It all seemed planned I thought. I could sense a smidgen of pride from Tina too. Once again, we ate the entire cake, although the cheesecake seemed more of a challenge. Misty opened her gifts and fawned over them as if they were the most special possibility of all. The rain had stopped, "why don't you put on your new shoes, and we can go break them in?" I suggested.

Misty looked at me as though I were insane, "I ain't wearing my best shoes out in that mess and mud, to get ruined," she had a point.

Instead, she put her new shoes in her bedroom, and then we all ran outside to play like we were kids again for the first time that summer. The creek was full from the rain and we splashed around. We had not been back to the waterhole since Sam's fight, and no one had even suggested it. The thought of splashing in that waterhole, which was full of Sam's guts, did not appeal to me. I was fine now with leaving the mysteries of paradise be.

I had bigger worries now than the waterhole. I stayed near the phone all evening awaiting the inevitable; a phone call from Pop. I kept my ears open for a ringing phone, and my eyes on the driveway for Pops truck. When the hand on the clock finally read nine, I figured that I was safe, for the day.

I spent my evening mental energy building my lie to cover my tracks. If Pop did call, I would try to intercede and make Grandma unavailable. If he did somehow tell her, I would assure her that I was with Mark and that this was all simply a misunderstanding. And if she confronted Mark, well, then I was screwed.

The next day Mark and I mowed with a fury to make up missing the previous day. All-day I spent imagining Pop making a house call to my grandmother. Tina trying to cover for me, and inadvertently making the situation worse. We didn't pull onto the farm until after dark that evening, and to be honest, I would have rather mowed through the night than to walk into that trailer.

It was Friday night, and the one night my grandmother would excuse herself from my grandfather for an hour or two. Grandma was a devout Seventh-Day Adventist (SDA), and sundown on Friday night marked the beginning of her sabbath. Every Friday night, for as long as I could remember, Grandma would get out an Ellen G. White book, and the bible, and hold a family devotion to begin the sabbath. When I walked through the door, they were all sitting in the living room waiting for me.

Completely forgetting the devotion tradition, my mind assumed the worst. My thoughts spiraled out of control concerning what had happened, and what would happen. No one got up from their seats as I entered the room, and no one said a word. I could feel all six eyes staring me down, judging me.

"You're late," was all Grandma said.

Grandma strictly forbids working on the sabbath. I explained that it was an hour's drive home from the last job site. I waited for the hammer to drop. "Well, go get cleaned up while Misty re-heats your dinner. You can eat in the living room while we worship," Grandma commanded.

I took a quick shower while deducing that Pop had not made contact. When I re-entered the living room it felt a little brighter, and I looked forward to the food that Misty had prepared, and the story Grandma would share. Tomorrow was Saturday, and it was my birthday.

I had spent so much energy trying to make my sisters birthdays special, that I had all but neglected my own. My big plan was to go buy myself a mountain bike from Walmart for my birthday. I did not realize that my birthday was on a Saturday. Just as Grandma forbids work on the sabbath, she also forbade shopping, or anything else other than worship or rest. It was fine, I would get the bicycle the following week, no big deal.

Saturday afternoon, while my grandparents napped, Misty and Tina sneaked to make my birthday cake. I could easily sense that they were trying to make up reasons to get me out of the house, and so I figured I would happily oblige. From the front yard, I noticed that Mark's truck was gone, and I couldn't help but wonder if he were off mowing somewhere without me. He was not quite as devout as his mother.

It was a typical sweltering July afternoon. My skin was leathered from working long days in the Florida sun, but I still sweat as though it were my first time in this temperament. I stopped in Uncle Mark's back yard to spray my head with the water hose in hopes of cooling down. While I was spraying water onto a bush waiting for it to cool down, I noticed both lawnmowers parked under the shed. Any sense of betrayal I felt vanished, and I wondered what fun he might be into today.

A nice breeze kicked up, and the enormous elder oak tree leaves rustled as they sang in unison. I decided I would go put my feet in the creek and sit and read a bit. I grabbed a random book about The Beatles from Mark's double-wide trailer and made my way down to the creek.

It was a beautiful, but boring day. As I flipped through The Beatles book, which was essentially a picture book, I considered what it meant to be thirteen. I was a teenager now. What was expected of me? Had anything changed? What should I expect from others? I somehow knew that the coming school year would be different, perhaps even transformative for me, but I didn't know how. Part of me wondered if I should be celebrating such a milestone in a grander fashion than spending it at Bristow Farms with my feet in the creek. As if there were another option. As I daydreamed of possibilities, I leaned back against the trusty oak tree and closed my eyes.

Sometime later, I was awakened by splashing water. I wasn't sure how long I had been asleep, but I knew it was significant because the sun had fallen behind the wooded swamp. Tina was laughing hysterically at herself for spraying her sleeping brother with her water gun. I was forced to assure her that there would be vengeance. "Come on home, your cake is ready," Tina squirted me one last time, and I jumped up and playfully chased her towards the house.

Once we came around the shed, I noticed that there were two vehicles in the front yard. For a split second, my heart sank. I quickly realized that the full-sized van belonged to the Ridgards. Partially hidden behind the van was Uncle Mark's truck.

The Ridgards were an SDA family whom we had become close with during our time attending church school. They were an immigrant family from Jamaica, and my sisters and I were obsessed with their accents.

The Ridgard family had two children our age. Tybalt was a couple of months older than me, and Abigail was the exact age as Misty; to the day.

Since we had returned to public school, the Ridgards would often take my sisters and I to church on Saturdays. When they dropped us off, they would visit with my grandmother for a bit while the kids played outside. When we missed church, as we had today, they would often stop by on the way home, and fellowship with Grandma, sharing the sermon and catching her up on church news.

Tybalt ran out of the screen door, and met me by the garden with a high five, "Happy Birthday Tommy," he said grinning ear to ear.

It was nice to hear the event recognized by someone other than my sisters. "Thanks man, how was church?" I asked reflexively.

Tybalt just shrugged, and we chuckled to one another as we ran off to join our sisters. We played together for a few minutes in the front yard until Mark beckoned us onto the porch. Entering the porch, I immediately noticed that cake and ice cream were set up, and ready to serve. I guessed this was a party, perhaps a rite of passage. Everyone sang Happy Birthday to me, and then I made everyone else sing it back to my sisters and Abby, and then we finally enjoyed the desserts.

Everyone stayed on the porch for about an hour. It was probably the coolest option. Eventually, the Ridgards began saying their goodbyes, and we all made our way back into the yard. Before the family could load up into their van, Mark piped up, "Tommy, you left something in the back of my truck."

Mark was never very delicate or timely, but everyone stopped talking and moving as if I needed to correct the mistake this second. Half annoyed, I let down the tailgate of the truck to find what I had so selfishly left. In the back of Uncle Mark's truck was a brand new blue Huffy twenty-one-speed mountain bike. I was shocked stiff. It was the exact bicycle that I was planning to get. I had tried to show it to Mark once before, but he did not seem the least bit interested. I wanted to hug someone, but I didn't know who. "That's from Uncle Mark and us," Grandma ended my stunned silence.

Before I even touched the bike, I said, "I will go get the money."

Mark removed the tobacco pipe from his mouth, and knocked it against the tire of his truck, "it's a gift, you deserve it, keep your money."

I wanted to cry. No one had ever bought, or given me anything nearly this big or meaningful. Instead, I pulled the bike from the back of the truck, and rode a small lap around the vehicles, switching through the gears, while my sisters jumped and cheered. The Ridgards, who had been sitting in their van waiting to leave during all of this, suggested that after church next Saturday, we all go for a bike ride at their house. Surprisingly, Grandma agreed that we could.

Thirteen turned out to be a special birthday after all. Perhaps not as big or extravagant as most of my schoolmates, but meaningful for me nonetheless. I had now achieved half of my summer goals. I owned a means of transportation more than a pair of shoes. I could go anywhere now, and quickly. I could ride my bike down the tracks into town. Although, now that I knew that I could easily drive into town, that might be better I thought. In two weeks, if we did not receive a surprise phone call, I would be on the road to Wisconsin. Two weeks was a long time to hold one's breath, but every day got a little easier.

The call never came. Perhaps Pop hadn't seen me driving alone after all. Or maybe he had simply forgotten. I got to go to the camporee in Wisconsin. The week-long camp went by fast, and the two weeks that followed before school started back, crept by slowly.

The first day of school we took the bus. I stepped off of the bus and surveyed what the eighth grade might feel like. I immediately spotted Pop and attempted to shrink my size to that of a typical eighth-grader in hopes that he would not see me. I ventured through the crowd following the group of equally confused students figuring out where they should go. Suddenly I heard Pop nearby and calling my name, "Tommy, how was your trip?" he beckoned.

"Real good Pop, the adventure of a lifetime," I assured him.

"Good...good. I saw you getting off of the bus, and I was a bit surprised that you didn't drive today," Pop said matter-of-factly.

He waited just long enough for my heart to sink, to make me pay for my sin, and then he shot me a wink. Nothing more was ever said of my maiden voyage to Miller's supermarket.

2020

I pulled the rental car into the parking spot closest to Subway. I had been cursing myself for going cheap, and renting the small sedan every time I banged my head of the roof getting in or out of it. I imagined how much more productive I might have been if I had rented a truck instead. Might've been worth the extra hundred dollars.

I spotted Tina and her three children exiting the Family Dollar at the other end of the sidewalk. Perfect timing, I thought, as I checked the time on my wristwatch. It was two minutes until 7 p.m. which is when we had agreed to meet at Subway for dinner. I knew that Tina would not come to the farm, and I was surprised when she suggested meeting in Hawthorne.

I stood in front of the sandwich shop watching Tina, and her family walk my way. Her oldest daughter, Addy was already taller than Tina, who was at least 5'7" herself. I wondered how old Addy was now? Impossible that she was a teenager I thought. The walk was further than it appears, and I became uncomfortable watching them, so I shifted my gaze to the grocery store. It was no longer Miller's. Hitchcock's had bought the store some time back, although as far as I could tell, the only thing that had changed was the name on the sign.

When my family finally approached me, I immediately embraced Tina awkwardly, and then inspected the children more closely. "Let's see here then, you must be Dana, and that would make you T.J." I intentionally confused their names, "wow you look so different!"

Addy chuckled slightly at my cheesy joke, but Dana and T.J. just stared at me with contempt. "Ok, ok, tough crowd," I ruffed T.J.s bright red hair, and Tina giggled.

Addy and T.J. had bright red hair like their mama; which made sense. Seeing Tina's children made me miss my own. My daughter Madeline had a hint of red in her hair too that I could not explain. Family, friends, and strangers would often comment on Madeline's beautiful red hair. I did not think of her hair as red and corrected everyone that her hair was in fact brown. But, a few times, when she has been in the right lighting, I could see the red shining through. I love red hair, but for some reason, I could not accept my own daughter being blessed with it.

"Are you guys hungry?" I said turning towards Subway.

"The kids are begging for Judy's," Tina sighed.

I turned back towards the kids, "Ok, who is Judy?" I tried to hide my exhaustion.

"Pizza," Addy chirped, pointing back towards the Family Dollar.

I shrugged at Tina, "pizza does sound better, lead the way!"

Immediately I noticed that Dana and T.J.'s entire demeanor changed from annoyance to exuberance. I laughed to Tina, "when charm doesn't work on children, try pizza."

I spent the wait on our pizza trying to remind the young children who I was, and how cool I am. I was at least partially successful and pulled them into my shenanigans, which Tina tolerated. Once the pizza arrived and the children were distracted, Tina and I engaged in polite small talk. I told her what I had been up too, and what I was doing at the farm. She got me up to speed on all of the family gossip. She told me that she was getting married in the following spring, and how much she enjoyed living in Ocala. Suddenly the pizza was gone, and I had the full attention of the children again. "Perhaps we should have some ice cream too," I suggested to the children but looked to Tina for permission.

Once dinner and dessert were done, we made our way back out to the sidewalk. There was a light sprinkling rain, and it had cooled down significantly since we entered Judy's. We stood facing out toward highway 301, and watched the rainfall for a minute, while I was playfully pushing T.J. into it. The kids were having a good time now, I could tell. Uncle Tom doesn't get many opportunities to build memories with his nieces and nephews, so he has to make them count. In this instant, he was buying their affection. "Why don't we go into Family Dollar, and see if they have any toys?" I barely finished my thought before all three children were running that way.

Tina and I walked slowly, winding down our evening. By the time we reached the store, the children were at the counter with their chosen toys, and I met them with my credit card. They were delighted, but Tina reminded them one by one to say thank you as they left the store.

"Where are you parked?" I asked Tina.

"Way back down there in front of Subway," she responded.

It really wasn't that far, but I spotted a red minivan parked right next to my rental. "Ah, I parked right next to you, that works out."

The kids jumped into their assigned seats focusing on their new toys, I strapped them in and forced their attention back to me with a tickle each. I closed the van door, and made my way away to the driver's side where Tina was standing. She was staring at my rental car.

"Not my car," I assured her, "I feel like I should be carrying it on my back," I joked.

As though she hadn't heard me, she did not say a word, flinch, or smile. It was then that I noticed that she was looking into the passenger window. As I stepped beside her, I saw what she saw. In my passenger seat, were the two framed photographs. The one Uncle Ray had given me, and the one from the hotbox.

"Oh yeah, I was going to offer you one of the pictures," I said as I went to open the door to retrieve one.

As the door cracked open, an enormous gust of wind blew in from the north, against the storm, and nearly ripped the door from my hand. The door was not open an inch when unexpectedly Tina kicked the door shut. Stunned, I turned around to face her, and she finally looked me in the eye for the first time that evening. I could sense a mixture of fear and anger. I did not break my gaze. This was the most real moment of the evening, and I wanted to understand it. Tina saw my confusion and looked away back into the window of my car, confusion forming in her face too now.

Finally, not knowing what else to say, I explained "the girl is Grandma, when she was young, the Uncle Ray made the frames from her childhood home," I tried to explain.

"I know, I don't want it," was her only response.

I wanted to ask why the outburst? Why did you kick the door? Instead, I figured it was better left alone. The kids were sitting in the van and were undoubtedly paying attention now. We had a fairly decent evening, and I didn't want to ruin it.

"Ok, no worries, I just wanted to offer," I told her as I gave her a goodbye hug, "it was good to see you and the kids."

I opened her car door for her and waved bye to the kids one last time through it. Tina stood in the open door with contemplation written on her face. "Don't give it to Misty either. Misty may have forgotten, but *she* hasn't. If I were you, I would destroy them, but I can't. Please get rid of them Tommy," Tina pleaded.

She wasn't asking me to, she was begging me. With that, she got into her drivers' seat, and closed the door. I stepped onto the sidewalk, and watched them pull away. Why would I destroy them? Who is *she*, and what *hasn't she forgotten?*

16

Kidnapped

1995

I had saved all summer and survived my driving expedition. Tomorrow, I would be joining Tybalt, and several other church children riding (not driving) from Gainesville, Florida to Oshkosh, Wisconsin for an international camporee with ten thousand other campers. The only other two places I had even been outside of the Hawthorne zip code, was Lakeland, Florida (3hrs), and Raleigh, North Carolina (8hrs). Oshkosh would be nearly a twenty-hour drive.

Our halfway point was not really halfway at all. We spent the night at an SDA church school campus in Calhoun, Ga. This meant we would have thirteen hours of driving to do the next day. I didn't care about being cooped up in a van because I was with friends, and I was experiencing something new. I felt bad for leaving my sisters on the farm alone, but they were used to spending the days alone now anyway, and they took their own medicine at night.

I bought a couple of ten-cent postcards on the journey and filled them out. I never actually got a chance to mail them, so I would give them to my sisters when I returned home. One was from Misty Falls in north Georgia that I figured Misty would get a kick out of. This trip was full of firsts for me. First time to Wisconsin, Illinois, Kentucky, and Tennessee. First time being away from family for an extended period of time. First time meeting many new friends from around the country, and indeed the world. And even my first kiss. I had no desire to return home now that I knew what freedoms and adventures existed away from Bristow Farms.

Just as quickly as the trip had arrived, it was over. The only proof that I had ever left Hawthorne that summer was a handful of stories, a couple of polaroid pictures that had been given to me, and a page full of mailing addresses. I would treasure them forever. As we crossed the Florida state line someone said *welcome home*, but for some reason, I no longer shared that sentiment. How could I return home with so much left to explore, and so many friends yet to make? I did not see how an opportunity such as this would ever present itself again.

My attitude did not improve much by the time we passed the Hawthorne city limit sign. I was excited to see my sisters, but mainly to tell them about my trip. School would start in a couple of weeks, and I figured to fill my time until then writing to my new pen pals. As the Ridgards' Peugeot van pulled across the railroad tracks, I sat in the back row of seats playing with Tybalt, determined to not let the trip end until it absolutely must.

A couple of minutes later, we pulled into the front yard, and I was forced to face reality; I was home. Only once I had slid out of the van did I notice the Lexus sedan parked between the van and the house. Curiosity piqued, I snatched my bags and gear from the back of the van quickly. I did not spend nearly enough time thanking the Ridgards for letting me tag along, or saying goodbye. Just as quickly, my mind was already forgetting the trip. Who could we possibly know that owns a Lexus? Why are they here on a Monday evening?

Realizing my rudeness, I turned to wave farewell to the Ridgards as they backed out of the driveway. With that final symbol, the trip was over. So was the summer, I thought as my shoulders sank a little. I reached down to regather my gear when I heard the screen door to the front porch opening. My first thought was that it was surely my sisters coming to interrogate me about my cross-country trip. As I picked up my last bag, I realized that I had not heard the door slam, as it would have if it were my sisters coming to greet me. Strange for Grandma to be awake this time of day I thought, but then again, it looks as though we have company.

I finally accepted that I had to go inside, and turned toward the house, and my greeter. It was not my sisters, and it was not my grandmother. Dr. Laura stood holding the door open for me, and I stood holding my mouth open for her. I was shocked to see her standing on my porch. She was certainly the last person that I expected to see today. I had not seen Dr. Laura in almost two years, but I was very happy to see her today.

Time had leveled the playing field. Even in her glossy black high heels, I now towered over Dr. Laura by several inches. This realization boosted my confidence. However, I was suddenly quite conscious that I had not showered in several days, nor was I wearing shoes. She somehow looked even more beautiful than I recalled. I hoped that I no longer appeared a little boy to her either. Something had certainly changed, or become more prevalent, but I wasn't sure what. I wondered if it had something to do with last week's kiss. Perhaps, I had been poisoned.

Suddenly, I realized that I had not said anything, and was still staring at the doctor drooling. She wasn't even sweating. How is it possible that she was sitting in the hotbox in August, without sweating? Stop thinking Tom, say something. She beat me to it, "Welcome home Tommy," she smiled and invited me inside.

Dangit, I thought, still the little boy. "Hey doc," I mumbled in disappointment as I lugged all of my gear onto the porch at the same time.

I dropped my stuff in the corner in no particular fashion. Laura must have sensed my disgust with how she had regarded me because she stepped up her charm. She made a show of sitting down in a poor rusty metal folding chair as though it were the most comfortable chair she'd ever sat in, "how was your trip?" she couldn't stop smiling.

Before I could answer, I realized that my sisters were still nowhere in sight. Instead of simply plopping down in my Granddaddy's rocking chair, I attempted to mimic her graceful movements. Tommy would have reacted to this realization, but Tom was mature enough now to play her game. I would know what she had to share with me soon enough. "Wisconsin was amazing, and the journey was epic," I grinned.

Dr. Laura must have noticed that my words were different or picked up on a variation in my voice, because her smile turned into a smirk, "I am glad you enjoyed it Tom, I'm jealous."

That's right, I'm Tom now. She sat as though she expected me to say more, but I would not share every detail with her. I was not a little boy anymore. I had to leave some mystery. "A house call in August, your presence must be serious," I couldn't help my cleverness.

It was then that I noticed that Dr. Laura had positioned her chair directly under the ceiling fan. Her hair was pulled into a tight bun, making the breeze from the fan virtually unnoticeable. Suddenly, she looked far less comfortable than I was. Her smirk was gone. "Yes, I am sorry to say, that it is quite serious," she began as she leaned toward me in her seat a bit.

Now I was uncomfortable. Not because of the nature of her visit, but because Laura was inches away from me, and I was certain that I could smell myself. "Tom," Dr. Laura took a pause to make sure she had my attention, "your sisters are missing."

I sat silently for a second digesting the information. Of course, I knew where they were. How could I not? How could anyone not? These people were still not paying attention to us. Not really anyway. Clouds of anger formed in my mind. This woman, as beautiful as she may be, had never taken us seriously. I reminded myself that she was only here because she had to be; not for me.

"Both of them?" I asked.

Dr. Laura nodded informatively.

"How long have they been gone?" was my next question.

Dr. Laura picked up a file from under the chair, which I had not noticed before, and shuffled through some papers. The clouds grew darker, she didn't even know how long they had been missing. "They were reported missing last Tuesday. So, officially, they have been missing for six days," she gently closed her file.

I jumped out of my chair. "Six days!" I shouted, "freaking idiots!"

I wasn't referring to my sisters as idiots, but every adult that we had ever trusted. I was already through the screen door moving at full speed. I was halfway across the first garden when I heard from behind me, "Tommy, where are you going?"

There is Tommy again. Liars and idiots, I thought.

I didn't stop running until I reached the empty abandoned farm-house. I finally came to a halt under the pecan tree to catch my breath and think on what I was about to do. Obviously, I had to look inside of the house. I was certain my sisters were in there. Then what? What if they were inside of the house? What are the chances that they would be alive? If they were alive, what condition might they be in? What if *she* were in there? Would *she* let them go? *She* had never kept them for so long before. If *she* thought that *she* was protecting them, surely, *she* would want them to have food and water, right?

Lost in my thoughts, and the general eeriness of the house itself, I did not hear the quiet Lexus pulling up behind me until it was already there. My anger was dissipating, and I was glad that she followed me. I wasn't scared of the house, but I was scared of what I might find. I was glad that I would have someone with me. I was happy that it was her. I heard Laura getting out of the car, and waited for her to join me, without immediately acknowledging her presence. As she stepped up beside me, I never could have guessed her first words, "do you realize that you aren't wearing any shoes?"

I couldn't help but laugh. I looked down at both of our feet. I suppose that you can tell a lot about a person by their feet. At thirteen years old my feet were already toughened from daily exposure to the elements and environment that made Bristow Farms. Laura's feet, although covered with fancy dress shoes and stockings, I imagined were quite soft and pampered. "I assume that you knew that you were coming out here today. Why did you dress this way?" I pointed her out head to toe.

Laura chuckled, "I suppose that it is important to look professional," she offered halfheartedly.

Looking back to the farmhouse I responded rhetorically, "important to who?"

She joined me in examining the farmhouse from under the pecan tree. "So, this is the house I have heard, and read so much about?" I wasn't sure if she were asking or stating.

"Yup," I said wondering what exactly she had heard or read.

"What makes it haunted?" she asked me pointedly.

I considered several responses, but in the end realized that I had no idea what made it haunted, "I dunno," I honestly said.

We regarded the house in silence a moment more. "You know, we aren't complete idiots, the police checked this house, and have searched the entire farm; multiple times," Dr. Laura informed me.

Clearly, they had not found my Misty and Tina, but I wondered aloud, "did they find anything?"

Laura hesitated, "nothing that could help find the girls. They brought out dogs, but your sisters' scent is all over this property. The only thing that the trackers could agree on, is that their scent does not leave the farm. That leads the police to believe that either they are still here somewhere, or they left in a vehicle," Laura stopped talking to allow the information she had shared to sink in.

I understood her words, but I could not understand what she was really implying. After a moment of consideration, I mustered the courage to ask, "what does that mean?"

Laura looked at me now with compassion and honesty in her eyes, "it means this might not be a best-case scenario; the story might not have a happy ending. If they are still on the farm, they are either the world's best hiders, or, God-forbid, they may be buried," Laura paused out of respect, "if they left the farm in a vehicle then we have to worry about who they are with, and what their intentions are."

My eyes began to leak, and I took a step towards the house, hoping that Laura would not see. This somehow seemed more serious than a ghost story. As long as the girls were physically safe on the farm, then we could figure it out, as we always had. But, if they were gone or GONE, then what would I do? What could I do? They had to be here.

"Listen, Tom, we do not have much time. The only reason that I got to talk to you first is because you are a minor, and a ward of the state, but the police are coming to talk to you very soon," Laura said.

The first question in my mind formed based on the context of Laura's previous words, *why would the police want to talk to me?* I suddenly felt guilty, but I had no idea why. I had seen enough police drama on NBC to know how these things worked. "Am I a suspect?" I asked trying to sound not guilty.

Laura stepped up beside me again, "No, you are not. We know that the girls were here after you left, and we are confirming right now that you were in fact in Wisconsin for the past eight days," Laura pointed me toward the farm entrance.

I could see the Ridgards' van parked in the road, and a police car blocking the railroad crossing. I understood that the police were corroborating with the Ridgards that I had been out of state with them the entire time. A sense of relief followed by embarrassment came over me. Mostly I felt embarrassed for my sisters. They still weren't recovered from the last incident over two years ago. This would surely compound rumors and feelings.

In that moment, I knew why I felt guilty. Not because I had done anything sinister to or with my sisters, but because I had abandoned them. I knew the challenges they faced on the farm unlike anyone else, and yet I still chose to leave them here alone. No, I definitely should not have gone to Wisconsin. Or perhaps I should have taken them with me. I have no idea how I would have done that, but where there is a will there is a way.

I looked back to the railroad crossing and noticed the vehicles moving. I figured now that they were finished talking with the Ridgards, that I was next. "What do they want to know?" I begged Laura.

"Tom, first you have to understand, that we just want to make sure that you are ok. Are you in a situation in which you believe that you may be injured or disappear too?" Laura asked me.

I looked at her as though she were crazy. Why in the world would she be worrying about me instead of my sisters? "I am fine," I reported rather coldly.

Laura nodded her head knowingly and rubbed my back. It didn't feel as though she were treating me as a child. It felt relaxing. "The police will want to know if you have any idea where your sisters might be, or why they have left," Laura removed her hand from my back.

I stared at the farmhouse, "if they aren't in there, then I have no idea where they could be," I offered.

Dr. Laura took in the house again, "why do you think that they would be in there?" she asked.

I was torn. Tell Laura my truth, and seem crazy, but get to spend a lot more time with her. Or, provide a lesser truth, and protect myself. I decided to start here and see how it would go. "They believe this house is special. They like it here," I didn't lie.

"Is the house special?" Laura asked a little too quickly.

It was apparent to me that her question was prepared. I pointed to the farmhouse, "that house was built immediately after my family got off of the boat from Ireland. We built that house before we even owned the property, if you believe my Grandma, it has been standing longer than this town. Five generations have survived everything that this cold world has thrown at them because we have been able to take refuge here. So, to answer your question, I dunno, but it seems pretty special to me."

It was Dr. Laura's turn to appear taken aback. I was not sure where those words came from, but they felt good. The real question was, did I actually believe them? In my peripheral vision, I could see the police cruiser now making its way up washed-out road. I was unsure if it would turn towards the hotbox, or if they saw Dr. Laura's Lexus at the farmhouse.

"If your sisters left of their own accord, or with someone, do you have any idea why, or with whom?" she asked a little more quickly.

I stood there dumbfounded. I was thinking whilst shaking my head no. In reality, that wasn't entirely true. My sisters had probably left on their own, kind of. They were probably with someone too or something. There was no way that I convince Dr. Laura, or anyone else of this madness, without seeming insane myself.

I was still standing there shaking my head no when the police car pulled up beside Laura's Lexus. Laura touched my shoulder, "I will be right back," with that she made her way to speak with the officers.

I followed her with my eyes until the officer met my gaze. I nodded at him as Laura began speaking and returned my focus to the farmhouse. The police had checked Laura said, but my gut told me, that if my sisters were alive, they were inside of that house. I felt a strong urge to go inside of the house. Almost as if the house or my sisters were begging me inside. I began inching towards the house, completely forgetting about Dr. Laura and the police officers.

Just as I grabbed a hold of the corner of the front porch to pull myself up, Laura grabbed my shoulder. Surprised, I fell back into her collapsing us into a heap on the ground. By the time I realized what had happened, Laura was sprawled out on the ground, and I was on top of her. I looked down at her, saw the horror in her eyes, and immediately jumped up. The officers had noticed the commotion and were making their way towards us, but in no rush. I put my hand out to help Laura up, and she accepted. "I'm sorry, you startled me I guess," I tried to explain.

Laura was brushing grass and leaves off of her skirt when the officers reached us. She assured them that we were fine, and asked for a moment more of privacy. The officers returned the way they came content with small talk, and their Slurpee's. "I guess you were right, I am not dressed appropriately for fieldwork," Laura conceded with a laugh.

I laughed a little too. I was happy that she wasn't angry about being knocked down. Her smile disappeared, and she asked a question, "did you not hear me calling you?"

I knew what she must have meant, but I had not heard a word. I was focused on getting inside of the house. I knew that my sisters were inside waiting on me. "No, I'm sorry, I didn't. I need to check inside of the house..." Laura intentionally cut me off.

"We will. But first, the police just want to ask you a few questions. I have confirmed that you are not a suspect. However, they believe you know more than they know concerning Misty and Tina's whereabouts. Just be truthful, and tell them what you know. It will be ok. Do you understand?" she asked.

I nodded my head and eyed the house one more time as we turned back to the short walk to the officers. More or less they asked the same questions that Laura had. Only without nearly the depth or concern. The only question that interested me was their last one, "Do you have any idea where your sisters may be?"

I sighed deeply in frustration, and turned back toward the farmhouse, "Yes, they are in there," I raised my voice slightly.

The two officers looked at each other with confusion, and then at Dr. Laura. She clarified, "the house has been searched and cleared, but Tom believes that they could be in the house now. Would it be ok if we took a look?"

The officers didn't seem bothered by my claim. It was late enough in the evening now that, if you were acclimated, the heat was tolerable. We all made our way up to the house. I easily pulled myself up onto the porch, as I had dozens of times before. Laura hesitated, and I am sure that once again she was wishing that she had worn different shoes. The officers stood behind Dr. Laura indicating that they had no intention of going into the house unless necessary. Laura was still on the fence, "are you sure it is safe?" but I don't think that she was asking me.

"Ya'll can wait here," I didn't wait for permission.

The door was locked. I moved to the window and peered in. There was no sign of my sisters, and everything appeared as it had always been. I put my leg over the window sill to climb in, "What are you doing?" Laura begged.

Before I could answer the officers felt the need to assert their authority, "come on down from there son."

"The door is locked, I am just going to open it," again, I didn't wait for their approval, and quickly disappeared into the house.

To appease the adults, I immediately went to the front door and opened it from the inside, so that they could see. Laura was standing directly in front of the door, still on the ground in front of the porch. I waved to her, and immediately felt silly. She waved back. One of the officers loudly slurped the last of his Big Gulp. "One second," I motioned to Laura.

I turned back looking into the kitchen, and the living room. From where I stood, I could basically see the entire house, except for the upstairs. I reminded myself that there were no stairs, so the likelihood that they were up there was slim. They didn't seem to be here. How could that be? Where else could they be? I stood there for a long minute racking my brain, and searching for a clue. I could feel the adults growing impatient outside. In an attempt to plead with my sisters, the house, or the spirit I called out, "Misty! Tina! You can come out now!"

I heard some movement behind me outside. I looked back through the doorway to find that the officers had crowded in behind Dr. Laura for a better view. Once they realized that I was safe, annoyance set in on their face. "Come on out of there boy," the previously quiet officer piped up.

The look on Laura's face told me that I could take as much time as I needed. It didn't really matter. I had already internally resolved to return as soon as they left anyway. I would keep coming back every day until my sisters returned because what else could I do? I ignored the officer's command and turned back into the house. I stepped further into the kitchen, and called again, "Tinaaaaa."

A bellow came from outside, "hey kid, I said get out of there, now!"

The officer struggled his way up onto the porch. I felt the house shudder a bit. So did the cop. The difference was, I knew that he had not caused the shake. The movement caused the officer to stop on the porch, but shout another command, "this house isn't safe, you need to get out of there now!"

I could feel a presence growing enraged. It may have been the police officer, but I didn't think it was. I had a feeling that the only way to figure out where my sisters were, was to bring this spirit out. I'm not sure why, but I smiled sinisterly at the cop and said, "this is my home, you get out!"

The officer stepped into the doorway and opened his mouth to speak, but another voice beat him to it, "Tommy, come home," a little girl's voice shouted softly.

The cop was still frozen in the doorway, but now I could see his partner climbing onto the porch the best he could. The officer was now in the house, but could not decide if he should search for the girls, or run for his life. I could only barely tell that Laura was still on the ground behind the law. I turned back to the kitchen as said, "it's ok, come on out," I wasn't sure if I was talking to my sisters, or someone else.

I could have sworn the girls' voice came from above, and so I raised my eyes to search the loft. It was then that I noticed the large wooden beam that ran across the kitchen ceiling no longer read *come home*. Instead, it read *get out*. Before I had a chance to heed the warning, I spotted what looked like red hair hanging over the ledge of the loft, "Tina," I shouted.

As I tried to step forward a hand grabbed my shoulder from behind, "stop," commanded the cop.

As quickly as he had grabbed me, his hand was gone. A mighty roar echo throughout the house, *GET OUT.* A hurricane-force wind moved through the kitchen but didn't move me. I turned in time to see both officers flying from the house over Laura's head, and falling hard under the pecan tree. As I saw them hit the ground, the door slammed hard.

I looked back up to where I had seen my sister's hair. It was gone. The beam now read, *Come Home*, again. It was then that I understood that my sisters were alive. They were still on Bristow Farms. Now I hoped that they would come back soon.

17

The Happy House

I opened the front door to exit the farmhouse. Not more than thirty seconds had passed since their abrupt eviction. The officers were still sitting on the ground trying to shake off their fall, and perhaps understand what had happened. I wasn't worried about them at all. I was worried about Dr. Laura who still stood frozen at the base of the porch, eyes wide, but now filled with tears. I knew what she was feeling. She shifted her gaze slightly upward toward me, and the tears broke down her cheeks. I wanted to smile to reassure her, instead, I said, "I am ok. They are ok."

It didn't take much convincing to get the police officers to leave Bristow Farms. They had the information that they had come for to include in their report. Both cops seemed content not to discuss what had happened in the house with me or Dr. Laura. They knew what I had known all along; that no one would ever believe them.

But now, Dr. Laura would believe me. She was ready to talk. Her mind was open, and so was her heart. "I guess you gotta be getting back to Gainesville?" I asked sheepishly.

She didn't even pretend, "I am not in any rush. I am hoping that we can talk more. I need to better understand what just happened here. All off of the record of course. Are you hungry?" she asked.

Dr. Laura took me to dinner at Sonny's Real-Pit-BBQ in town. At the restaurant, we engaged in mostly small talk. I told her about my trip. When I tried to pay, she kissed me on the cheek and called me a gentleman. "The state of Florida is paying for this meal," she preserved my ego.

It wasn't until the drive home that we broached the subject of the farmhouse and possible spirits. I could tell that she was finally genuinely interested in what we had been experiencing on the farm. It was a great relief to finally share in all honesty the phenomenon which we had endured the last few years, and not feel as though I would be labeled as a crazy person.

I started at the beginning the best I could. I told her about the pond and the calling. I told her what I had seen the nights leading up to, and the night that Tina stabbed me. And how I didn't think that it was Tina who stabbed me at all. I told her about the connections with the cat and the bull, and about the scar. The part that I really tried to help her understand was that whatever, or whoever was doing this did not seem to mean the girls harm. Quite the contrary, the presence appeared to be trying to protect them. I had to walk Laura through the events several times, pointing out how we believed we were being protected.

She didn't understand why a ghost would want to protect my sisters, but not me. I told Laura that I believed it wished to protect me too, but in the beginning, it perceived me as a threat for endangering Tina with shenanigans. I think that she expected me to protect my sisters.

"Who is she?" Laura finally asked the obvious question.

"That's the question. I don't know for sure, but I think it might be my Old Grandma. She was Grandmas' mother. If it is, then it is her when she was young. Old Grandma died in her eighties, so I am not sure why she would be young. Of course, all of this is equally as crazy," I joked.

Dr. Laura thought for a second, "is your Old Grandma buried on the farm?"

I had already checked, "no, she is buried in the cemetery in town."

"Do you know any cause she might have to be haunting that house, this farm, or your sisters?" Laura continued probing.

I thought for a second, "I'm not sure she is haunting anything."

"Maybe I didn't mean haunt, but why is she still here instead of, well, there, resting" Laura tried to be sensitive.

I didn't have an answer for her, but we continued chatting on the front porch well past sundown. I knew she would leave soon, but I didn't want her too. I even considered pretending to be scared so that perhaps she might stay. I knew that would be a stretch. The conversation did not seem to be in any risk of dying out until she said, "wow, what a crazy day huh. I wish I had some wine."

I chuckled uncomfortably, "yeah, unfortunately, Bristow Farms is dry."

Laura giggled suggestively, but then said, "oh no I didn't mean I would drink here with you."

My heart sank a little as Dr. Laura stood up. "Will you be ok here," she looked around, "alone?"

I stood too to remind her that I was bigger than her now, "oh sure," I shrugged.

We stood under a bare-naked light bulb, which was wobbling from the ceiling fan, making the light bounce in her eyes. The contact seemed to linger for longer than one might have expected. We now understood each other, of that I was certain. She reached out and touched my arm, "I am sorry," was all she said with her words.

I opened the screen door for Dr. Laura more than six hours after she had done the same for me. It had indeed been a day for the ages, I thought. My thoughts were interrupted when Laura turned back to me, at the bottom of the stairs, and asked, "what was that?"

"I didn't say anything," I responded hoping that she hadn't heard me swooning.

"No, listen. Do you hear that?" we were both as silent as possible.

I held my breath. It was difficult to hear anything over the crickets, and millions of other insects that gathered nightly at the lamppost on the corner of the carport. I tried to listen harder, if that was possible. I could hear something besides bugs now, faintly. It sounded like laughter. Far in the distance were two girls giggling. Laura and I looked at each other in bewilderment. Could it be? Have my sisters come back, I wondered?

"Come on," Laura said motioning me to the other side of her car.

I wasn't exactly sure what she was doing, but I wanted to go along for the ride, literally. When she passed washed out road, I knew for certain that she was headed for the farmhouse. Sure enough, as we passed the pond, up ahead, we could see light coming from inside of the house. I instinctively grabbed Laura's leg, and she jumped a little, "are you sure you want to do this?" I asked.

She gulped but kept her foot on the gas. She did not pull up to the pecan tree. She cut her lights off, and then the engine behind the bales of hay next to some blackberry thickets. I couldn't help but laugh aloud, "if you think that she doesn't know we are here, you are mistaken."

We sat in the car for a moment watching the house. There was light pouring out of every window, downstairs and upstairs. Now that we were closer, we could also hear music coming from inside too. After taking in the spectacle occurring in the lively farmhouse for a minute, Dr. Laura looked at me in awe. I didn't know what to say either. This was unlike anything that I had ever seen before. "Um, I have a feeling that I know the answer, but is there electricity hooked up to that old house?" Laura deadpanned.

"Nope," I responded dryly.

"What should we do?" she asked with a hint of desperation in her voice.

I sighed aloud, "you're the adult with a PhD, you tell me," my words came out snarkier than I meant them too.

She didn't seem to notice, "should we call the police?"

I looked to her in exasperation, "that is the absolute last thing that we should do."

I began opening my door, "what are you doing?" she grabbed me.

I smiled bravely at her, "I think that we should get a closer look," I stepped out of the car, and for some reason softly closed the door.

Laura followed suit and met me at the hood. "Listen. No matter what happens, my sisters and I will be fine, I promise, but you cannot enter that house," I searched her eyes for clarity, "do you understand?"

She nodded, and her eyes told me that she understood the consequences if she did not heed my advice. I stepped off towards the house, and Dr. Laura grabbed my hand to follow. Just hours ago, I might have been shocked by such an action, but now it felt natural. We snuck, although I realized that we were not really sneaking, up to the pecan tree.

From the tree, with the house lit up like Christmas, we had a clear line of sight to everything that was happening in the house. The first thing that I noticed was that the house appeared a hundred years younger than it had earlier that day. The front porch no longer sagged under the weight of years of oppression and neglect. The windows had been restored with beautiful glass panes, and they were halfway open, accommodating the cool evening breeze. Through the open doorway, I was astounded to realize that all of the clutter, junk, and trash that had accumulated over the decades had disappeared. In the kitchen, I could see a simple but sturdy farm table surrounded by handmade chairs. On the table, there sat a fresh hot pecan pie with steam rising from its trimmings.

A young lady was busy wiping bowls and pans when a little girl ran into the kitchen and tugged her gown. The girl had bright red hair like Tina, but was much younger, and could not be older than five. The lady scooped up the girl and began swirling magnificently to the music around the table, both giggling with delight. Unintentionally, I gave Laura's hand a happy squeeze. I felt her looking at me now, but I couldn't help but beam. Finally, I looked down at Laura to find her still staring at me. We both smiled. She diverted her attention back to the house. Laura whispered softly, "is that Tina?"

I responded, "no, I don't think that it is," but I also felt as though I needed to clarify, "that child is much younger than Tina."

"I know, but if Old Grandma is sixty years younger in the house, perhaps Tina can be five years younger," Laura made a valid point which I had not considered.

Almost as though someone were reading our minds, a movement crossed the living room and joined the two strangers in the kitchen. It was Misty and Tina. They appeared healthy and happy. Misty tried to stick her finger in the pie and earned a smack on the wrist from the lady. She took Misty by the hand, and then also grabbed the smallest child's hand. The little girl took Tina's hand, and Tina held Misty's other hand. Then they all began skipping around the table counter-clockwise singing *ring around for Molly, Molly wants a dolly*.

I cocked my eyebrow, and looked to Laura who appeared equally as confused. The incident was far too interesting to try to intervene yet. When the dance was finished, the lady began speaking softly to the girls. All three girls looked up to her in admiration and respect. The woman appeared to be repeating something. Then the girls tried to recite the saying, getting a little better, and a little louder each time. However, I could not make sense of what was being said. Once the girls had perfected the words and were being praised for their accomplishment, Laura looked at me and repeated: *Lá breithe shona duit.*

"I think it is Gaelic. I had a boyfriend in college who was trying to learn the ancient languages. I am fairly certain it means Happy Birthday," Laura offered.

I didn't know what Gaelic was, but I didn't want to seem even more ignorant than I already did, so I nodded in agreeance. When I looked back into the house, the woman was placing five candles into the pie. I gave Laura's hand another squeeze indicating how impressed that I was that she was right. As soon as the woman lit all five candles, Misty, Tina, and her began singing *Lá breithe shona duit Molly*.

When they finished the song, the little girl closed her eyes hard for a long moment, and then, with all of her might, blew out the five birthday candles. The entire house was darkened once more. No sounds of happiness rang from the interior. The house again was alone, sad, and sagged in despair. Fear of the unknown wrapped around us with the darkness and Laura clung to me tightly.

We waited for something else to happen with the house. We watched it intently for a long time. Maybe the house would light back up, and we would find the girls sitting at the table enjoying their pecan pie. After a few minutes, I really just hoped that my sisters would emerge unscathed.

We were so focused on the house that when a noise came from the other side of the tree, we were both startled, and we fell down in a scramble, landing in a pile of fallen pecans. It was a partly cloudy night, but the moon was shining bright. We could now clearly make out sobbing coming from the direction of the pond.

I stood slowly and then helped Laura to her feet. She was still wearing high heels, and it did not seem to be a lesson she was taking. Once she was on her feet again, she kept my hand. I crept towards the crying, but Laura was hesitant. The sobbing had become more of a wailing, that neither of us could believe would come from a child.

The moonlight reflected on the water of the pond. In the night light, the pond appeared clearer, and much more beautiful. By the time we reached the barbed wire fence, the wailing had stifled. Then came the call. "Come home Molly. It's time to come home!" the woman repeatedly shouted from the shore.

Then came a tug from behind us that caused Laura to launch herself into the barbed wire fence cutting her arms and legs so that she bled badly. I turned to find Misty and Tina standing calmly behind us in their nightgowns, "it's time to go home," was all that Tina said.

Dr. Laura was in shock. Perhaps it was from her cuts, but more likely, the event had proven more than she could handle. I helped her out of the wire, and into the passenger seat of her Lexus. Once I loaded the girls into the back seat, I started the car and drove us home. Everyone was completely silent for the short drive, except for Laura, who was trying desperately not to whimper.

We all settled in on the front porch, and Misty gathered the first aid kit. Dr. Laura was not seriously injured, she was just a bleeder. Once I cleaned the blood from her and nursed the nicks and cuts, she was as good as new; physically at least. I was just about to demand some explaining from my sisters when the front door opened, and Grandma peered onto the porch. All of us, including Laura, looked at the tired old woman, "the girls are home," was all that I said.

Grandma looked over the girls from a distance and offered, "oh good. Did you girls have fun?"

Misty and Tina responded in unison, "yes ma'am."

"Good. Ya'll don't stay up all night now ya hear," with that she withdrew back into the trailer.

Grandma had not even acknowledged Dr. Laura who now shot me a wide-eyed look of astonishment. Maybe Grandma was delusional. Maybe she was just exhausted. Most likely she knew where the girls were, and what was happening all along, I thought. I turned my attention back to the girls, "well, are you going to tell us about your adventure," I asked somewhat mockingly.

"Old Grandma said it wasn't fair that you got to go have fun for a week without us," Tina started.

"So, she invited us to stay with her for the week," Misty finished Tina's thought.

"We had so much fun!" Tina chimed back in.

I smiled at them because I knew that they had. Laura spoke to the girls for the first time, "but the authorities searched that house multiple times. We looked in there today, and you were not there," she needed it all to start making sense.

There was a significant pause as the girls thought of how to explain, "we weren't in that old house. We were in it when it was a new house. Not brand new, but in 1928," Misty said proudly.

Laura was stunned, and it wasn't getting any better. "Wow, what was it like?" I asked.

Tina chirped up, "it was so cool! You could get a Coke for a nickel," she jumped up with excitement.

"We only walked into town with Old Grandma once, to get some supplies to make Molly's birthday pie. It was very different back then, but there were a lot more people in town, and they sure seemed kinder," Misty's simple description fascinated me.

"Who is Molly?" I finally was able to ask the question that had been gnawing on me all night.

"Molly is Old Grandmas' daughter," Tina said as if it were logical.

"But our Grandma is Old Grandma's only daughter," I corrected my little sister.

"Nuh uh," replied Tina, "and she looks just like me!"

Laura was beginning to accept this new reality, I thought, because she no longer appeared utterly shocked by every word that emerged from my sister's mouths. "Where is Molly now then?" Laura asked logically.

"She's in the new house," Misty said as though she were annoyed with re-explaining the obvious.

"In 1928," Laura nodded confirming that she understood.

It was then that I noticed something sticking out of the pocket of Tina's nightgown, "What is that?" I asked pointing to the object.

Tina smiled, and pulled out an ugly little doll from her pocket, "Molly gave her to me, she is going to get a new one for her birthday," Tina held the doll up to the light, "her name is Dolly."

I took Dolly from Tina's hands and examined her closely. The doll wasn't soft or cuddly, and I found the look of her quite repulsive. Sure, I was a boy, but I had held my sister's dolls before. This felt different. Her head, body, legs, and arms did not feel like the smooth plastic I expected. I turned the doll to Laura so that she could see it better, "it feels gross," I added.

Laura took the doll from my hands to examine closer. "That's because it isn't made of plastic. My mother collects dolls like this, it is called a composite doll," Laura smiled at Tina, "this is a very special doll. Take extra special care of her," she handed Dolly back to Tina.

When Laura turned back to me, she added, "in that condition, this doll could be worth millions of dollars," she apprised me, but I knew that Tina would never give up the gift from her friend.

The mood shifted slightly, "Tina, do you know what happened to Molly?" I asked.

"What do you mean? Nothing, she is at home," Tina sounded worried.

"Yes, but why doesn't she exist in our lifetime?" I asked delicately.

Misty and Tina looked at each other in a manner that I knew they had not considered the implication before I had mentioned it. I could tell that neither of the girls had a real answer to the question, but finally, Tina said, "maybe she just likes 1928 more."

I accepted that the mystery may never be solved, but had to ask the obvious question, "what will we tell the authorities? They are going to want to know where you guys have been, and why. I don't think that we can tell them you were in 1928."

Laura intervened, "I can take care of that, but we have to agree on a few things and get our ducks in a row. The police will have to come out tomorrow to make sure that the girls are here, and they will follow up with a few questions. I will remind your grandmother that she sent Misty and Tina to stay with their Aunt Molly while Tom was away. I just need you girls to do me one favor: please stay in 1995."

2020

I slowly pulled back onto Bristow Farms not long before dark. Tomorrow morning, I would leave to return home to Kansas City, and my own children. I had arranged with Uncle Ray to spend the night in his camper, but instead of taking the left turn onto his property, I turned right onto washed out road once more. A moment later I found myself parking beneath the big pecan tree. I approached the cattle gate where Uncle Ray had found me on arrival a couple of days before. I immediately spotted Philip coming across the cow field in his Ram pick-up truck and waved to him. He turned in my direction.

He pulled the truck up to the gate parallel, indicating that he had no intention of disembarking. "How was supper?" he asked.

"Not bad. Tina took me to Judy's pizza. It was my first time," I explained.

Philip just nodded his head knowingly as he liked to do. "I'm taking off first thing in the morning, back to Kansas City. I'm not sure how quick I will get back, but I sure appreciated your help today," I thanked him once more.

"Ah, I didn't do nothin," was his way of saying welcome.

"Uncle Philip, I asked you a question when I was a boy, and I asked you the same question today. Both times you gave the exact same answer, but I don't understand what you mean. How was the old farmhouse dangerous?" I pleaded.

I could sense an uneasiness come from his truck, "ah, it was just old. Needed to come down," he tried to skirt the question.

"I really don't think that is what you meant by dangerous," I confronted him.

He snapped his head in my direction at my challenge but didn't say anything for a minute. "Don't you remember any of that stuff that happened to you, and your sisters when you was a young'un?" he asked in annoyance.

I answered honestly, "only vaguely, but it has been coming back to me since I have been here."

"Yeah, that ain't no surprise," Philip added.

"Do you think the house was haunted?" I asked him.

"It was somethin' alright," was all he would say.

It was becoming quite obvious that my uncle would not be volunteering any information. I would have to pull it from him. Fortunately, the Army had trained me for such interrogations. "Uncle Philip, do you know who Molly is?" I asked a little more forcefully.

I could tell that he was trying hard not to react. He went back to staring out of his windshield towards the pond. "Well, not really no, but I heard some things when I was a boy," he started.

The hair on my arms stood up. Maybe we were about to solve a thirty, no a ninety-year-old mystery.

Philip continued, "I suppose there ain't no harm in tellin you what I heard, but it ain't no fact though. Ain't no proof. Ain't nobody alive could confirm nor deny the stories. Ya understand, this is just me and you talkin. It stays here. Ain't no need to go stirrin up old drama," he looked at me hard for assurance that I understood.

I nodded my head in agreeance.

Uncle Philip maintained his stare out of the windshield of the Ram, and never once looked at me, but continued his story, "When I was a young boy, I would sometimes hear my mama, and daddy fightin late at night. Sometimes I would hear the name Molly. Yo mama, my sister, was supposed to be the oldest child, but I ain't so sure that's the truth of the matter. I may have had an older sister named Molly. Of course, I never met her. I guess she must have died before I was born," Philip removed the worn-out John Deere cap from his head and wiped his brow.

What he had just told me made sense based on what I had remembered from my childhood, but why would that be a secret? Why wouldn't Old Grandma, or Grandma want us to know about Molly? "Do you know how Molly might have died?" I asked Philip.

"Well, yeah, that's where the story gets a little thick. Or maybe I should say stories. I heard several over the years helping the neighbors in their fields. The most likely explanation is that she got the fever or pox and perished, but you know how folks love their drama," Philip paused as though that were the end.

I hung on the gate, and his words, "Well, what stories did you hear?" I begged.

"Ah well, one rumor I heard was that in 1928, that was about two years before yo mama was born, on Molly's fifth birthday, she wandered out into the pond and drowned."

My pulse was racing. How could I just be learning about this? I could barely breathe and for once, it had nothing to do with the humidity. All of the pieces were falling into place. This story was starting to make sense. In that moment, I couldn't help but wonder what had ever happened to Dr. Laura. Surely, she would love to know who Molly was, and what happened to her, almost as much as my sisters. I had a feeling that somehow, the girls already knew. The pond, the calling, the protection, the house everything was aligning for me after almost thirty years. Then I realized that there was more, "you said there were other stories?" I urged Philip to continue.

"I never cared much for the story, and never harassed my mama about it at all, what's done is done. But yo mama, she always wanted a sister. It made her mighty mad that my mama wouldn't tell her about Molly. When your mama got growed up, she went down to the hospitals and the county and searched everywhere for information about Molly. As far as the state is concerned, Molly never existed," Philip described.

"No, that ain't right. I know for a fact that Molly was alive in 1928, I saw her," I blurted out without thinking.

Uncle Philip again snapped his gaze to me. I really couldn't qualify my statement more than that, but I think he knew what I was referring too. For the first time in many years I could see Molly vividly in my memory. Almost as much as her hair made her stand out, her smile was infectious. In that moment, it occurred to me that my own daughter Madeline had an identical smile. Side by side in my mind I could see Molly and Madeline's matching smiles. The thought made me smile and shudder at the same time.

"Yo mama was sure of it too. She never stopped looking for anything that might tell her something about Molly. I never had the heart to tell her what I had heard. The second story is what you might refer to as ne-farious. Rumor had it that a month before my mama married my daddy a traveling farmhand, with fire for hair, came to Bristow Farms. He and my mama started getting mighty close, and one night her daddy caught them a canoodling up in the hay rafter of the barn. Her daddy threat-ened to beat the farmhand if he didn't leave, and never return. Well, mama married daddy, and nine months later a baby was born," Philip paused.

"Molly," I looked to Philip for confirmation.

"Yup, she was born in the farmhouse, there weren't any doctors out this way back then. She never went to Gainesville to get recorded in the census neither. I guess everything went fine for the first few years, but then Molly's red hair started to come in. Now we come from the Irish folk, but you would be hard-pressed to find any other red hair in our family..."

My thoughts momentarily drowned out my uncle's voice as I tried to recall if there were any other redheads in our family. The only obvious answer was my sister Tina and her children. If Molly is real, then I suppose that makes another. Then I thought of another redhead: my daughter Madeline; who also has a matching smile.

"...Daddy just knew that Molly had to be the farmhand's child, but mama denied it with her entire being. That was when daddy started drinking. There was a prohibition, but you could get the shine from just about anywhere around here. Daddy could be a violent man. He whupped me all the way up until I could whup him back. Anyway, the story goes that daddy sent word for the farmhand to come help with some cattle, and he came. Daddy got him way out back there in the old wooded swamp and kilt him, and buried him past the water table line," Philip stopped to read my reaction.

If he was going for effect, it was working. I never knew my Uncle Philip to be a storyteller, but there I was, hanging on his every word.

"You know, I never told nobody this, but I always believed that's why the water in the swamp is black, but it comes out red. It sounds crazy I know, but I ain't seen nothing like it nowhere else neither," Philip waved his hand in the air either swatting a mosquito or the notion.

I thought back to the water hole, "wait, is it red because of his hair or blood from the murder?" I asked seriously.

Philip must have thought I was joking because he just laughed and continued his story, "either way, getting rid of the farmhand didn't make daddy no better. He still just got drunk, and angry every night. Truthfully, I believe if mama could have borne him a child right then and there, that might have been the end of it. But he just couldn't bear the idea of her loving that little girl so much, cause you see, she was a part of the farmhand too," Philip checked to make sure I was tracking.

"Every evening, the first thing daddy would see coming in from the fields was that head of bright red hair bouncing up and down waiting to see her daddy. The problem was, my daddy knew that he wasn't her daddy. Her daddy was rotting in the swamp. It hurt him something fierce. That's why he would often rush right past her on the way in, and grab the bottle instead," Philip explained.

There was a moment of silence, and sadness between my uncle and

I. "So, on Molly's fifth birthday, mamma made plans to go into town to get some supplies for the kitchen. Daddy was suffering from a hangover, and in his stupor, he agreed to stay with Molly that morning while mamma ran her errands. At that age, children are so full of energy and curiosity. I couldn't tell you if she drove daddy mad, and he did something on purpose, of if it was just a case of neglect. When mamma got home that afternoon, daddy was passed out on the porch, and Molly was never seen again. Mama was furious and threatened to call the sheriff on daddy. He swore he hadn't done anything, but mama noticed that daddy had done changed his clothes. What he had been wearing that morning was a hanging up on the old clothesline, soppin wet," Philip pointed to an imaginary clothesline that once ran between the big oaks by the pond.

I was stunned silent. Was it possible that there had been two murders on Bristow Farms, and one of them a child of the family? How could anyone keep something like this covered up? "So, Old Grandma blamed Great Granddaddy for Molly's death, but she stayed with him?" I asked Philip trying to make sense of how this could be.

"Oh, folks in these parts didn't divorce back then like they do nowadays. Mama didn't have no other way of managing this big farm by herself, and she wouldn't never get no help from any other man in town if she up, and divorced daddy. Even if he was a murderer. So yeah, I reckon she stayed. And two years later she gave birth to your mama, which is when daddy stopped drinkin, and started goin back to church," Philip rationalized.

I couldn't make sense of it, "if people were telling this story, then obviously they knew something had happened to that child out here. No one wanted to investigate?" I begged aloud.

"Rex Hill was a tight community back then. Folks kept each other's secrets. Wouldn't have done nobody any good stirring up trouble like that. Certainly, wasn't gonna raise the dead. I guess they had their reasons, Lord knows that mama had hers," Philip concluded.

"You never told your mother that you knew any of this?" I asked Philip.

"Naw, what would be the point of that?" he seemed sure.

"So, she carried that awful secret by herself her entire life," I said aloud, but not to necessarily to Philip.

"I guess so," Philip realized.

"Maybe that is why she stayed after she died. Maybe Tina reminded her of Molly, and she couldn't bear to lose another child. Or maybe she wanted to finally be happy here with her first daughter?" my mind was exploring the possibilities as wild as they seemed.

"I don't guess I had ever thought of that," Philip said.

His words reminded me that he was the one to tear down the farm-house, "seems wrong to have taken that from her," I pointed the accusation towards Philip.

Philip didn't flinch, "you mean the house don't ya?"

"Yes. So, what if all of this were true. It is sad, certainly, but I don't understand how the house was dangerous. Especially, once my sisters had left," I stated.

Philip looked very surprised by my harsh words, "your sisters didn't leave."

I was confused, "what do you mean? Misty lives in New Mexico and Tina lives in Ocala," I reminded the old man.

"Sure, they do now, because they were released when I took down the house," Philip told me.

The look on my face told my uncle that I had no idea what he was talking about. "That's right, you were already in the Army by then. Misty graduated that year after you left for the Army. She had plans to join the Marines. She had signed the paperwork and everything. Then just before she was scheduled to ship off to Paris Island for boot camp, she came down with a sickness which voided her contract with the military," Philip explained.

I vaguely recalled something about that, but I didn't understand what it had to do with the house.

The following year Tina graduated high school and got accepted into college down at the University of South Florida in Tampa. That summer she was packing her things, and had a freak accident, and broke both of her legs," Philip recalled.

How had I forgotten this, and what did it have to do with the house?

"Every time one of the girls made plans to leave the farm, something terrible would befall them. It was the house, or mama trying to keep them here. It did the same thing to your birth mother when she tried to leave the farm, and take you kids with her. She couldn't stay here. That's why she left ya'll here with my sister to raise. I didn't put it all together until your sisters got stuck here. That's when I decided that I would tear down the farmhouse. Mama couldn't move on; this farm, her family, and that house is all she ever knew. But the world is different now than it was then. She stayed here even after daddy died, knowin she couldn't run this farm alone, but she always believed that Molly might return one day. She conditioned your mama to stay too, even though she probably never knew it. But you kids have your entire lives ahead of you. I had to stop it, and so I did," Philip suddenly seemed sad and tired.

I reached over the gate, through the window of the truck, and grabbed Philip's shoulder. I gave it a little shake and a pat. It was the closest thing to a hug, or affection that we ever shared. I spent most of my life believing that the old man didn't love anything except his cows, but now I knew the truth. He had destroyed an important piece of Bristow Farms to save my sisters, and maybe stop a curse.

Philip started his truck, "yeah, well, those are the stories anyway. Don't matter if they're true now, what is done is done," when he looked at me, I noticed that his eyes were wet; it might have been sweat, "I gotta get on to the house before I lose all of my light. It was sure good to see ya Tommy. Gimme a holler when yer headed back this way," and with that he shifted the truck into drive, and pulled back across the field.

I stayed on the gate until the sunlight completely disappeared, letting the mosquitos have their feast. The story was running on loop in my head. I was adding my own pieces of information to what I had learned. I wondered if I should have told Philip what I knew, but I figured he knew more than enough already, and probably more than he had told me. Finally, a small breeze kicked up across the pond, which provided momentary relief from the blood-hungry insects. In that instance, I knew what I had to do.

Bristow Farms, and Old Grandma had suffered their tragic history long enough. I made my way back to my rental car. The house had been demolished for over fifteen years, my sisters had escaped their prison, but Tina had immediately recognized the piece of wood in my car. It seemed like the wood recognized her too. I saw the fear in her eyes. I might never know what changed for her, why she no longer loved the spirit or the house, but I suspected that she had just reached a point of feeling trapped.

I opened the passenger side door and took out the two framed photographs. The wood felt ice-cold, I assumed from the air conditioner in the car. As I carried the frames across the short distance to their final destination, they suddenly jumped from my hands. The frames both bounced around on the ground as if an earthquake were happening. It was then that I realized that I was standing directly where the farmhouse stood for over a century. A breeze kicked across the landscape begging me one last time *Come Home*.

Now was not the time to second guess myself. I snatched up the two frames and ran as fast as I could to the pond. I expected something terrible to happen, but the frames, the pond, and the farm remained calm. I held up the pictures one last time and admired them. I spoke, "it's time to say goodbye, it's time to go home."

With those final words, I hurled the frames deep into the middle of the pond and watched them sink. Part of me was afraid they would float on the surface, waiting to be reclaimed by some unsuspecting family member. I imagined Old Grandma, and Molly being joined together at least, and Molly finally getting her new doll. When I was satisfied that it was over, and nothing more was happening, I left.

18

Going Home

I pulled off of Bristow Farms before dawn without saying goodbye to anyone. After my talk with Uncle Philip, I may have been worried that I wouldn't be allowed to leave either. I had a long drive to Kansas City, so I hoped that the Bristow's would understand. I was halfway to Georgia, and on my second cup of coffee when I found myself regretting destroying the vintage frames my uncle had made. The story Philip had told me was just that, a story, and nothing more. For eight hours, northbound on I-75, I replayed the memories and experiences from the weekend, of my childhood on Bristow Farms. By the time I reached Tennessee, I had already begun forgetting again. As I crossed into Kentucky all I was thinking of were my children and returning to Kansas City.

I had dreamed of raising my children on the farm and letting them have the similar happy experiences that I enjoyed as a boy since they were born. I had nearly forgotten the mysteries, tragedies, and happenings in Hawthorne. Time and distance hide the darkest secrets. We were happy in Kansas City, and that would be enough, for now.

A week after my return to Kansas, while I was at work, I received a text message from my daughter Madeline, who was at home.

Madeline: Daddy, we got a package from Aunt Tojuanna, can I open it?

Daddy: Sure honey, see you soon, love you.

By the time I got home from a long day at the office, I had forgotten the package but enjoyed dinner and a lovely evening with my family. At bedtime, I selected the book that we were reading and headed into Madeline's bedroom for storytime. Hanging above her bed was a beautiful black and white picture in a rustic looking frame. "Wow, where did that come from?" I asked my excited daughter.

The picture seemed familiar. Although I was certain I had seen it before, I could not recognize any of the people in the photograph. "Aunt Tojuanna sent it with this letter. Can I keep it in my room daddy please?!" Madeline begged.

"Sure honey," I appeased her as I took the letter from her hands.

Tommy,

I found this picture you must have accidentally left under the old pecan tree. It is a picture of your mama when she was a little girl, with her brother Carl, and their mama and daddy. There were two pictures, but I figured that you didn't need both, and so I sent the other one to Misty. I sure hope that you don't mind. We enjoyed the visit, and are excited to be getting you back.

Love,

Aunt Tojuanna

I remembered now that Uncle Ray had made the frames from the old farmhouse that my Grandma had grown up it. I shared the short story with Madeline. "This is a really special picture, be super careful with it, and treasure it always," I instructed Madeline.

I vaguely recalled an instance when I was a child, that Aunt Tojuanna had given me something special too. No, she hadn't given me anything, she gave something to my sisters. Something to help them understand how special family is. Was it a cat? I had a feeling that this gift was equally as special.

I hoped Madeline could appreciate the importance and significance of being responsible for such an important heirloom. She was obsessed with the picture and told everyone who would listen about it. She dusted it carefully every day. It was very sweet I thought.

In the following weeks, Madeline seemed to become more distant from her brother and I. She spent an unusual and inordinate amount of time up in her bedroom with the door closed. One evening, during a rare occurrence, Madeline came outside to play in the pool with the rest of the family. "Who is this gracing us with her presence?" I mocked as she came down the deck stairs.

She rolled her eyes at me the way tweens do and stepped out of the shadow of the house into the sun, and that is when I noticed. "Madeline Ann, you are in big trouble young lady!" I announced.

Madeline stopped in her tracks and looked at me in confusion and exasperation. "Who told you that you could dye your hair?" I demanded to know.

"I didn't dye my hair!" she cried examining her new color closely in the light.

I was shocked. Could it be true? Her hair no longer appeared brown at all or even auburn. It was no longer a matter of accents or highlights. Madeline's hair was now undeniably red; similar to Tina's, and identical to Molly's.

A month later, I entered Madeline's room again for storytime. She was sitting up in bed waiting for me, brushing her doll's matching red hair. "And who do we have here," I asked reaching out for the interesting looking doll.

As she handed me the doll, I noticed that it felt strangely familiar, "her name is Dolly. My friend Molly gave her to me," she said.

Profits from A Happening in Hawthorne shall be used to restore
Bristow Farms.
Thank you for your support!

SPECIAL THANKS TO:
Ray Bristow
Tojuanna Bristow
Philip Bristow
Misty Tompkins
and
Tina Glick

The Spirit of the North
From the Imagination of:
Madeline A. Wiggins
Written by:
Tom A. Wiggins
Illustrated by:
Aaron Anderson
Coming November 2020!!

See <u>tommystales.com</u> for more

Lightning Source UK Ltd.
Milton Keynes UK
UKHW020012290920
370698UK00012B/665